IT'S THE END OF THE WORLD AND I'M IN MY BATHING SUIT

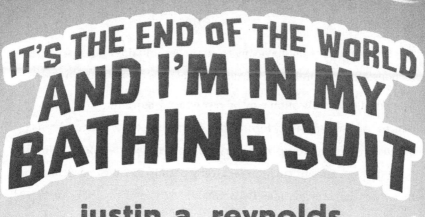

IT'S THE END OF THE WORLD AND I'M IN MY BATHING SUIT

justin a. reynolds

Scholastic Press / New York

To every kid who ever wondered if you have what it takes—you do!

Library of Congress Cataloging-in-Publication Data available

ISBN 978-1-338-74022-6

1 2022

Printed in the U.S.A.   23

First edition, April 2022

Book design by Stephanie Yang

An extremely brief note from our storytelling master, Eddie Gordon Holloway, who is about to hook you up:

Yo, what up! Before we jump into this story, first I'm gonna hook you up. I know, I know—you can hardly believe it, right? I mean, how many books have you read that took care of you off rip? But listen, don't even worry about it. Consider this a lil something to let you know I've got your back. You can thank me later.

Okay, so look—when someone sees me reading, I already know what's coming. It's always the same two questions.

Question #1 you could probably guess: "Hey, Eddie, what book you reading?" This one's easy to answer, although honestly it would be kinda weird to admit, "Umm, actually, I'm reading my own book."

Anyway, question #2 is where they try to get you. Smiling at you, they're all, "Hey, Eddie, what chapter are you on?" Now, listen, I have zero problem saying, "Oh, hey, I'm on chapter one." I mean, if I'm actually on chapter one. If I'm on chapter fifty-seven, obviously I say fifty-seven.

But let's be real, whoever is asking what chapter you're on is probably checking up on you. Which, you gotta admit, is a pretty solid teacher/librarian/parent/babysitter "Are you really doing your work?" question. And if you're only on chapter one, chances are you're probably not really working.

That's where I come in, ha. Since you're reading this book, the way I see it, that makes us friends, and since we're friends, I'm gonna hook you up, because that's what I do for my friends. So, yeah, instead of starting with chapter one, we're starting at chapter a hundred. Yep, you heard me—this story kicks off at Chapter 100. That way, if anyone asks, you can tell the truth. "I'm on chapter fifty-seven hundred" and you won't be lying. My mom says this is called being irreverent. I just call it doing what we want. So, ha! In your face, regular ole chapter numbers!

I told you I got you.

100

On the third day of summer vacation, I devised THEE perfect three-month plan.

It all started when I lost that entire first weekend (and half a Monday!) to more chores than should even be legal.

Including THE CHORE I HATE MOST...

Also known as The Chore That Shall Not Be Named.

Tuh, fine. I'll spell it.

L-A-U-N-D-R-Y.

Yep, the bright red cherry atop my dirty clothes pile.

Listen, I know what you're thinking: *What's the big deal with doing a little laundry, Eddie? The washer and dryer do all the work, right?*

WRONG!

Okay, technically, you're right; the machines are a lifesaver.

Mom made me watch this boring documentary where this kid my age—twelve, if it matters to you—is hand-scrubbing clothes against a block of wood for hours, which, ugh, brutal.

And you wanna know how you determined the clothes were clean enough?

When your arm fell off.

So, yes, it could be infinitely worse.

Buuuut even still, laundry isn't simply pushing the start button and kicking back.

Nope. It's a whole process.

First, you sort—whites, colors—and if you have my mom—reds and pinks, partial whites, pastels, earth tones, delicates, etc.

Next, you load the washer, which always, *always*, ALWAYS leads to a trail of dropped socks and underwear along the way.

Then while you wait for the "your clothes are ready" buzzer, you try not to get too caught up playing *Basketball Ballers 3K.*

And the dryer—sheesh, you better select the right temperature.

Choose wrong and your favorite T-shirt shrinks to a washcloth.

And can someone please tell me the point of folding and

stuffing your clothes into drawers if you're only gonna wear them again the next day?

Yep, that's why I devised THE PERFECT PLAN—and here it is:

I'm only doing laundry ONCE this ENTIRE SUMMER!

But, Eddie, how is that even possible? you ask.

I'll tell you how, my friends:

I'd wear every piece of clothing I had. That's right, all of it. That ugly Christmas sweater despite the fact that it's been hot enough to fry an egg on the sidewalk? Didn't let that stop me. Nope, I rolled up those scratchy green sleeves and did what needed to be done. That awful T-shirt my uncle got me with the dancing hippo sporting a backwards Kangol hat and Adidas shell-toes that says "I'm a Hip-Hoppopotamus" in huge gold letters? Rocked it last Thursday—The Bronster's still laughing about it. Those palm-tree Bermuda shorts that I stuffed in the back of my bottom drawer because they're wide enough to be a parachute? Um, wore those Tuesday—and the wind nearly carried me away. But it would've been worth it. Seriously, I could've floated to the moon and I'd still have zero regrets. Because if the plan's gonna work, well, I've gotta do whatever it takes, wear whatever it takes, end of story.

And according to my careful wardrobe calculations, all these necessary combinations would get me halfway through summer, with one last outfit:

My swim trunks. Just in time for Beach Bash.

After that, I'd throw everything into the wash and be good until school started back up.

Kinda brilliant, right?

Feel free to borrow it.

But, you know, only if you want to minimize your chores and maximize your fun.

I know what you're thinking: *But, Eddie, why would your parents let you get away with this?*

That's easy, because we made . . .

200

... the deal.

If I agreed to take care of myself for the whole summer—making my own sandwiches for lunch, cleaning up after myself, and we've already discussed doing my own stinking laundry (pun intended)—I'd be granted complete and utter freedom.

How could I pass *that* up?

It was the perfect setup.

A win-win situation.

My mom got to worry about me less all summer, and me—I got to be worried less about.

Everyone got what they wanted.

Everyone was happy.

I mean, with a deal that sweet, what could possibly go wrong, right?

7

Forty days later, I had my answer:

It's everything, guys. Everything's gone wrong.

Except not even that kinda-wrong-but-still-not-horrible way.

Not even that *okay, okay, this is definitely bad* way.

No, things got *bad*.

Really,

really,

really bad.

The type of bad where everything you thought

you knew, you're like, wait, now I'm not sure:

Your brain's all screwed up like, *Hold on, is up actually down?*

Oh, you think I'm exaggerating?

Well, fine, how 'bout you see for yourself?

But remember, I warned you.

300

It's like debating who's the GOAT—(a) MJ, (b) Kobe, or (c) LeBron.

Let's be real, it's crazy easy to make an impressive case for all three. For me, it's LeBron holding down that top spot—but the truth is, no matter how you slot them, you're not gonna be wrong.

And you're like, *Okay, Eddie, what's basketball got to do with anything?*

Everything, my friends. Everything.

Because when you're debating the (a) singing, (b) dancing, and (c) joke telling of Calvin Cleophas Eady III—

Also known as the man who married my mom not even six months ago. The dude I call Wanna-Be Dad. WBD for short.

—you're gonna feel super hard-pressed to pick which of his "talents" is the best. Let me clarify: *None* of them are any good. Like not even good-adjacent. In fact, the easier argument is that all three are *equally* awful, that their levels of lousy are a major toss-up.

But I know that's a cop-out. It's true, we all have that one friend who never decides *anything*, the friend who's always like, "Why do we have to choose? Why can't we just appreciate LeBron, Kobe, and Jordan and what they brought to the game, instead of arguing who's the best?"

Except if my Real Dad were here, he'd say, "Stop all that hemming and hawing and pick a side already. The best decision you'll ever make is to be decisive." Because the reality is: Whichever one you're leaning toward, you're 100 percent right.

But, Eddie, I'm still not quite following, why are we even talking about this?

We're talking about this because off rip, at an hour far too early in the morning for human interaction, let alone an entire *no*-talent show, WBD hits me *hard* with the Terrible Trifecta— (a), (b), *and* (c)—all at the same stupid time.

Dude, I haven't even picked the sleep outta my eyeball crevices yet. Like this can't be life.

"*Heyyy-ayyye, gooooood mooor . . . ninnng, buh-ud,*" sings WBD. I'll never understand how the guy manages to stretch a few syllables into a whole verse and yet he keeps pulling it off.

Normally, I eat this up, those random unexpected moments when my annoying brother, aka The Bronster, isn't around or is snoring in his dungeon lair. I savor each split-second morsel. But right now, I'd kill to have The Bronster here to deflect some of WBD's attention off me. And yes, I'm from Carterville, which is only twenty minutes from Cleveland, but no, my brother's name isn't actually "Bron"—which, I know, shocking, right? No, The Bronster is what happens when you mix equal parts *bro*ther + mo*nster* together. He's three and a half years older than me and basically treats me like I'm the baby troll he never asked for. Ever since Real Dad died almost two years ago, the Bronster's been meaner than ever. Mom claims it's just a phase, a teenager thing. But I have my doubts.

The point is, I want to *not* be alone with WBD bad enough to wish that my Neanderthal brother were around—which I gotta tell you, is not a wish I take lightly.

And all I really wanna say to WBD is: *Dude, can you just give me some time to wake up before you hit me with all your . . . your . . . WBD-ness?* Seriously, guys, I'm a creature of habit. I treat all mornings equally—which is to say, you know the day's started when you hear me trip down the stairs. Then I'm staggering into the kitchen like a newborn giraffe getting used to its spindly legs, my eyes cracked open just barely enough to identify large blurry objects, like the fridge, the kitchen table, and most walls.

That's the level I'm at right now.

So if this guy thinks I'm gonna be able to match his "cheerfulness" and "sunny disposition"—Mom's words, not mine—he's in for a rude awakening. *My* rude awakening, ha.

"I hope you slept welllll," WBD sings into a spatula, as if he and the spatula have worked out a deal—

WBD: *Hey, we both agree your primary job is flipping pancakes . . .*

SPATULA: *It's what I'm best at.*

WBD: *Okay, but in between those flips, you're also gonna be my microphone, got that?*

And as if that's not bad enough, WBD spins away from the food simmering on the stove, and is now gliding toward me and . . . wait a minute, I blink hard trying to bring WBD's non-spatula hand into focus because he appears to be holding something that I can't quite make out, but it looks like . . . oh, no. Oh, no.

It's . . . that stupid slotted spoon.

Every weekend, it's the same WBD show. He sashays around the kitchen, belting the wrong notes into his slightly melted plastic blue spatula . . . and then, when he thinks he's caught me off guard, he unleashes a surprise attack, thrusting some other kitchen utensil in my face—as if for even one second I'd pretend to sing along.

Last weekend, he offered me tongs. Today it's a slotted spoon.

"Coooomeeee on, joiiiin meeee, youuuu knoooow you wannn-aaa," WBD croons into his poor spatula, while extending the slotted spoon toward me like a bouquet of flowers.

I duck his second "mic" and slip into the pantry.

WBD watches me from the pantry door. "Oh, hey, question for ya, when you were taking the lawn mower out of the garage the other day, you didn't by chance rub against Betsy, did ya?"

Not this again. "No," I grumble. "I did not hit Betsy."

WBD smiles. "Hit? Who said anything about hit? No, I asked if you *rubbed. Rubbed.* Which is an easy incidental thing to do."

I shake my head as I snare the box of Froot Loops, aka the best cereal ever, from the middle shelf. "Nope. Didn't rub, either."

"See, it's just that . . ." WBD smiles harder. A thing he does when he's upset but doesn't wanna be. "Betsy is so special to me. The only thing I've got that was my dad's, so . . ."

"Dude, I did not hit, rub, or even breathe on your car," I say, squeezing past him to hit up the fridge for milk.

"I know it's hard getting the lawn mower out. It's tight in there. But I just . . . I'm just asking you to be careful, is all. Yeah? Can you do that for me, bud?"

Except there's no milk. Not *real* milk, anyway.

I whirl around to face my non-dairy tormentor. "Oat milk again? Don't you believe in regular milk?"

Oat milk's one of the many unwanted changes that came as part of the WBD package—apparently, the guy doesn't believe in cow milk.

"Oh, I believe, bud. I just don't think it's the responsible way to go if we wanna continue enjoying this planet for a long time, is all. Sustainable living and all that jazz? Sorry, bud." But he must notice my eyes glazing over, because he stops himself mid-speech and grins at me. "Gee, I'm sorry, boss. You know talking about the environment gets me all wound up, haha. Anyway, what's your attack plan for today? We're going to have a blast, pal!"

And I hear you already: *C'mon, Eddie, he's just . . . enthusiastic. But it's not that bad, is it?*

Oh, trust me, it is.

See, part of WBD's problem is that he doesn't know when to quit. Whether it's him pestering me about us *doing fun bonding things together*, or him insisting on raising his voice several octaves too high, making his already upsettingly pitchy "falsetto" so squeaky and so screechy that I swear he's Alvin, Simon, and Theodore's little-known, long-lost bro, Calvin Chipmunk, except with way less vocal range and you know . . . talent. On a good day WBD could *maybe* land on that big singing show *Vocalize*, on their "best of the worst auditions of the season" episode.

I can already hear the judges:

JUDGE #1: *Sorry, WBD, err, ahem, I mean Calvin, but it's a big no from me, dawg.*

JUDGE #2: *The only way I can properly describe what I just heard come out of your mouth is if that "nails across a chalkboard" sound and a squealing wild hog had a baby. You're that baby, Calvin.*

JUDGE #3: *If I had a time machine, I wouldn't use it for riches*

or power or celebrity. No, I'd use it to travel back in time before I had the terrible misfortune of hearing you sing.

    CALVIN: *So, you're saying there's a chance?*

Also, as previously mentioned, we can't forget WBD's equally bad dancing. I'll be real—and please don't take this the wrong way—but I assumed all Black people could dance.

Or at least had, you know, *rhythm*.

But WBD's definitely punched a body-shaped hole into that theory.

After his appearance on *Vocalize*, he could head next door and pop onto the *America Don't Got Talent* stage and not miss a beat—pun intended.

But not even (a), (b), or (c) can ruin my day. Because WBD's right about one thing: Today will be the best day of the summer, hands down.

And because I like you guys, I'm bringing you along for the whole awesome ride.

400

First off, there's the dragons.

I'm back in my room, going about my Saturday morning, devouring my bowl of Froot Loops and burning the entire city of Carcassonne to the ground.

I mean, I am going to TOWN, literally.

It's pretty flipping awesome.

Totally worth standing in line for two hours to make sure I got a copy of *Dragon Insurgents II* on release day.

Because now I'm just flying my happy dragon self back and forth across the medieval sky, breathing fire on anything and everything.

And while fire is shooting out of my mouth on the screen, I'm dreaming of something much colder in my real one.

Are you ready for this?

An extra-large Triple Berry Tongue Slap Your Brain Stupid Silly Super Slushie.

Seriously, I've been fantasizing about it for weeks now.

OMG, I'm actually salivating.

Like, if my tongue had a face, that face would be cheesing.

Lucky for me, in less than an hour, I'll be feasting on cup after cup of that red-and-blue-swirled frozen goodness.

Because today is Beach Bash.

THE BIGGEST PARTY OF THE ENTIRE YEAR.

A day when every Cartervillian—that's our town, Carterville—flocks to the shore for ultimate fun in the sun.

I'm dreaming of the juicy bacon cheeseburgers, ketchup running down my chin. Of neon fireworks bursting above us in the evening sky. And the live band music—I *love* the Calypsos. If I didn't know better, I'd swear I can already hear those soulful melodies wafting through the air . . . oh wait, it's because I *can* hear them. The Calypsos are our unofficial neighborhood band. *They're just a bunch of old people trying to relive their youth*, The Bronster likes to say, because it genuinely hurts his heart to see other people happy. The Calypsos must be warming up in Mr. Arnold's garage right now, running through one last pre-Bash jam session. They've been practicing in there for a month, playing a bunch of my favorite old-school songs, the ones Real Dad used to turn up on the living room speakers, swinging me and Mom (and even The Bronster) round and round until we were collapsed onto the floor, dizzy and howling with laughter. And then Real Dad would always make some cheesy dad joke and we'd all roll our—

Wait a minute. I think . . .

Tap, tap.

I think someone is at my door.

Knock, knock.

Yep. There it is again. Knocking confirmed.

Probably Mom asking me what soda I want to toss in our family cooler. Normally Mom's very anti-soda, but for Beach Bash she makes an exception. Like I said, it's a celebration.

"Eddie, you in there?"

"Yes, Mom."

My bedroom door opens slowly. "Eddie, I wanted to—"

Smiling, I interrupt her. "Cherry creme, thank you very much."

"Cherry creme?" Mom's forehead wrinkles in confusion. "What about it?"

My smile fades. "Oh, sorry. I figured you were gonna ask about soda."

"No, Eddie," Mom says. "Eddie, why are you dressed like you're ready for a swim? We're not leaving for the beach for a little bit."

Mom is referring to the fact that I'm sitting here eating my cereal in nothing but my pink-with-green-pineapples glow-in-the-dark swim trunks. I'm like the opposite of those signs you see taped to the door of the convenient store. *No shirt. No shoes. No . . . service.*

"Wait, wait," I say, throwing up my hands like I'm a school crossing guard. "I got it all covered!" I point down. "See!"

It was all worth it for this. Every mismatched sock combination, the pair of boxers that was too tight and the other pair that was too loose. All leading to today.

My absolute last item of clean clothing. All five of my dresser drawers? Totally empty. My closet rack? Nothing but unoccupied plastic hangers as far as the eye can see.

Mom glances down and frowns. "What am I seeing?"

"What are you seeing?" I repeat. "Umm, only the culmination of my most brilliant plan yet, *that's* what you're seeing."

Mom crosses her arms. She doesn't look convinced—at all. "Why do I have a feeling I'm gonna regret this?" she asks.

"You won't," I promise her. "All I need is two minutes to explain and then you'll see. Everything will make sense."

Mom lets out a sigh that could fill a hot-air balloon. "Okay, you've got two minutes to explain your brilliant plan. But I'm warning you, this better be good, Eddie."

A grin spreads across my lips, because "good" happens to be my middle name.

Okay, it's actually Gordon.

But c'mon—they both start with *G*!

All right, we're wasting valuable time here.

This is the part where I tell her the plan, minus the part where I complained about watching that washing board documentary, of course.

Except surprisingly, unlike most perfectly understanding and supersmart humans, Mom doesn't appreciate the brilliance.

In fact, she actually looks disgusted.

"Please, tell me you're joking, Eddie Gordon Holloway."

Uh-oh, she used my full name.

I don't think I need to tell you that's never good.

"I'm not joking. Look, we agreed that as long as I took care of myself and did my chores, you didn't care if—"

"Eddie, have you lost your whole mind?" Mom interrupts.

Okay, so maybe when Mom and I made the deal, I left out the part that I would only be doing laundry once all summer. But I was supposed to be taking care of myself—which means making these types of in-charge decisions. As long as I got the laundry done, I did my part, right?

I shake my head. "No, ma'am," I say. "Not my *whole* mind, ma'am."

And listen, I'm gonna be real. I don't normally say "ma'am" or "sir." Like at all. I mean, I'm an advocate for being respectful or whatever, but every time I hear someone say "ma'am" or "sir" it's like I'm ripped back in time to 1734. "Excuse me, ma'am, can ye point me in the direction of thou washboard? Sir, will ye please stop apologizing about my arm falling off? That's why I have two, am I right?"

But *this*—this is different.

Because in times like this, when the wrath of Mom is threatening to rain down on *my* village like dragon fire, swiftly ending my fun for the foreseeable future, I do whatever it takes to survive. Whatever's necessary to remind them that in the end I'm actually a pretty good kid.

I mostly stay out of trouble.

I get good grades.

At times like this, you can't hold back. You've gotta really pour on the parental respect. But I get the feeling I won't be going back to my dragon flying anytime soon.

"Where *is* your laundry right now, Eddie?"

I hesitate. *"Right now,* right now?"

A loud shriek erupts from my TV because, apparently, I forgot to pause my game, and my now badly wounded dragon has paid the price, yowling as she plummets to her doom. And yeah, it's kinda hard not to take this as a bad sign.

Mom shifts her weight to her other leg and is now posed in a position I like to call the "Boy, I'm not playing with you" stance.

To be fair, most days my mom's pretty reasonable.

I mean, you know, for an old person anyway (she's at least thirty-four!).

But when Mom shifts herself into *this* position, you've already lost. Because that sound you hear—that's the very last drops of her reasoning ability draining from her body. When you see this stance, it's best to tell the truth.

To get right to it.

To rip off the Band-Aid.

I nod toward my closet, and she follows my eyes toward its hollow, fake-wood double doors.

"The closet?" she confirms.

I nod again, prepared for a full-blown lecture. But entirely not prepared for what actually transpires next—

Because it all happens so fast.

Had I known what she was about to do, I would've stopped her, but . . .

"Eddie, all I know is you better . . ." She walks across my room and grabs the knob on my closet door—

"Noooooooo," I yell, flinging myself in Mom's direction. I attempt to dive in front of her, but I'm too late—

She turns the knob and immediately a low rumbling sound starts inside the closet.

Mom turns to me, a startled look on her face, her hand already pulling.

"Mom! No! Don't! Open! That! Door!" I exclaim.

But it's already done.

The rumbling rises to a sharp, roaring crescendo as an avalanche of my dirty clothes collapses, sweeping me and Mom off our feet in a wave of dingy tank tops and grass-stained blue jeans crashing to the floor.

I wish I was exaggerating, but it's true—

When the rumbling finally stops, there's not a single spot in my room that isn't blanketed in funky laundry.

And when I say *every spot* is covered, I mean it.

Because when I turn to Mom and see . . . when I see her . . . her current state . . . I am speechless . . . and not in a good way.

No, there is zero good about this.

Somehow, draped across the top of her head, are my dirty blue-and-white-striped drawers (leave me alone, they're *nautical*). Which is bad enough in itself.

Except these were drawers I'd worn on the very first day of my laundry plan.

As in forty days ago.

As in they've had over a month to stew and marinate in their stinky awfulness.

And all I can do is hope Mom doesn't notice. That she moves to stand up and my underwear falls harmlessly off her head, down her back, and onto the floor.

But as I watch her nose slide up and her face twist in sheer horror, I know my luck has officially run out.

"Eddie," Mom says without actually opening her mouth, her teeth gritted tightly together.

"Yeah, Best Mom in the Whole Wide World?" I say, trying to lay the charm on thick in one last desperate attempt to avoid punishment.

"Do I have your dirty undies on my head?" Mom asks.

I shrug. Force out a smile. "I prefer to think of it as my dirty undies have *you* under their bottoms," I say, adding a mouthful of uncomfortable laughter. *Hahaha . . . haha . . . ha.*

"Eddie Gordon Holloway, until you do every ounce of this laundry . . ."

I hold up my hands. "No, no, Mama, please don't say it . . . Please!"

"You will *not* be going . . ."

I desperately wave my hands in the air, like I'm an air traffic controller trying to guide a plane down for an emergency landing. "No, Mama, please! Please! Don't say it!"

"...to Beach Bash."

She said it.

And look, I'm not gonna be extra dramatic and tell you that my heart stops, or that all of a sudden it's hard to breathe, but ...

Okay, never mind, I *am* gonna be that dramatic.

I can't breathe, my heart's stopped, good night forever.

So long.

Farewell.

This is me, signing all the way off.

I'm dead.

500

Huh? What's that? You said, Eddie, I can't believe you're so dramatic?

Umm, sorry, I'm having a little trouble hearing you right now because I'm too busy TAKING MY VERY LAST BREATH ON THIS PLANET, thank you.

Listen, do me a favor, and just put me out of my misery.

Seriously, knock me out.

Hold my dirty nautical drawers against my face until I pass out.

I'm not kidding. Come over to my house—it's the one at the end of the cul-de-sac with the plastic pink penguins tap-dancing in bright red mulch in the front yard—yep, I said *pink* penguins— you can't miss it. If you somehow *still* can't find it, just keep walking until you feel your I'M SUDDENLY SO EMBARRASSED meter going crazy, and *ta-da*, you've found me.

I live at 325 Creekfield Court, which, by the way, is a street without a creek *or* a field. So that just goes to show you this whole world is MAD.

Now please hurry up and render me unconscious, appreciate it.

Seriously. It was *such* a brilliant plan.

THE PLAN OF THE DECADE—which is saying something considering I've only been alive for twelve years. So really, it might have even been the PLAN OF THE DOZEN YEARS.

Today should be about me lying in the sun, kicking back, spitting game to Ava Bustamante, who was already super hot but somehow, in the forty-three days since school let out, has become EVEN HOTTER. I'm serious. Yesterday, when she was delivering our newspaper to our front door, I nearly passed out from her HOTNESS.

Like I'm pretty sure the earth got confused and was like, "Wait, there's TWO suns now? How come no one told me? So, which one am I supposed to revolve around now?" That's how hot Ava Bustamante is. You can't look directly at her for too long without going blind.

And I would love to let you see this for yourself.

Unfortunately, I'll be too busy growing embarrassingly old and dying in a bed of stray dryer lint stuck between the wall and the washing machine.

600

Except wait, there's one—*achoo!*—important—*achoo!*—thing—*achoo!*—I keep—*achoo!*—forgetting: I, Eddie Gordon Holloway—*achoo!*—am severely allergic to—*achoo!*—failure.

It's true. I'm not making this up. Thing is: My allergy can flare up even when I haven't actually *failed* at anything, because it can sense my *maybe I'm just a loser* vibe. It *knows* I'm thinking about giving up. That I'm throwing a pity party and I'm the only one invited—and my allergies are like, nah, Eddie, we can't even let you go out like that, bro.

So let's not panic. I can still make this work. There's a solid move to be made here, I can feel it. But what? C'mon, Eddie, think.

Somehow, I've gotta convince Mom that I *need* to be at Beach Bash. That it's actually irresponsible of her to *not* let me go.

That denying me this party puts me—her own flesh and blood, her only decent son—at a difficult-to-overcome, lifelong disadvantage.

She has to think to herself: *Wow, if I don't let Eddie go to Beach Bash for the whole day, I'm clearly scarring him for life.*

Except Mom's way too smart to be persuaded by pretty words—yep, even mine. And she's far too suspicious of me and The Bronster to be fooled into changing her mind, which totally isn't fair. Sometimes she acts like *all* we do is plot and scheme.

No, if I'm gonna get through to Mom, I need an indirect approach. I've gotta make her feel like she's coming to this *Eddie's gotta be at Beach Bash* decision on her own.

But if she won't hear it from me, and definitely isn't gonna listen to The Bronster—not that he'd help me anyway—then who can I . . .

Wait, that's it. How did I not think of this sooner?

"Morrnnning, boss," I sing to WBD, as if I hadn't already seen him. As if I hadn't turned down his invitation to have a full-on slotted-spoon/spatula duet right here in this very kitchen. And yeah, the last thing I wanna do is encourage this man to sing . . .

but sometimes, to get what you want, you've gotta sacrifice, even if the thing you're sacrificing is your hearing. Because for my plan to have even the slimmest chance, I need WBD on my side. "I meant to tell you earlier when I came down—is it just me or are you looking even fitter than normal, WB—I mean, Calvin?" I flash him my brightest thousand-watt smile and the countdown begins. 10 . . . 9 . . . 8 . . .

"Who, me?" he asks, laughing and waving me off. "No way, but that's nice of you to say, Eddie. Very nice, haha. I certainly wish, but nah."

7 . . . 6 . . . 5 . . . My eyes are glued to WBD, looking for any clue, the smallest hint that my compliment's landed.

4 . . . 3 . . . C'mon, WBD, I know you felt that. I know you wanna, so just do it, man.

2 . . . Aww man, it's a no-go. It didn't work. He's not—

1 . . . And then it happens. I watch as he swivels toward our coffee cup cabinet, his back now to me, except I can just make out the move—if I weren't paying close attention I would've missed it, but there it is, subtle and small. WBD inconspicuously glides his flattened palm down the front of his shirt, a quick "gut check," a smile spreading across his face as he thinks to

himself, *Hmm, could Eddie be right? I* have *been hitting the bike path harder this month. All your hard work and discipline is paying off, Calvin. Keep it up, my friend. Bravo.*

"You're just being modest," I add, prepared to lay it on as thick as necessary, prepared to double-, triple-, quadruple-stack as many ridiculously thick layers of compliments as are required. Whatever gets the job done. Whatever punches my ticket to Beach Bash. "You should be proud of your hard work, Calvin."

WBD turns back toward me, two coffee mugs pressed together, looped on two fingers of the same hand. "Well, thank you, Eddie. That means a lot."

I nod. "Listen, I know I haven't always made it easy for you to be here these last six months since you and Mom got . . ."

WBD picks up my train of thought, as I knew he would. "Hey, I get it. Don't worry about it. This is new for all of us. And it's a big adjustment, my friend. Truthfully, I think you've handled it a lot better than I did at your age."

My eyebrows slide up my forehead as if to say, *Why whatever do you mean, WBD, please, tell me more.* "Wait, you mean you . . . ?"

WBD nods. "Yep, I have a stepdad, too. And I definitely wasn't excited about him moving into *our* house, eating *our* food from *our* fridge, and watching *our* TV." Calvin laughs, his eyes looking in my direction but not actually focused on me, as if he's left the present and is now back in the kitchen he grew up in, reliving all those memories, remembering what it was like to walk in my flip-flops. And okay, I admit I didn't expect *this*. That WBD would drop the whole *I know how you feel, I know it's hard, but I think you're doing great, I think you're great* routine on me. Sheesh, there's no way this guy is really *this* nice, is there?

I almost feel bad about taking advantage of him, but then outside our kitchen patio door a cloud slides away from the sun and a direct beam of sunlight pours through the glass, beams into my eyes, warms my face, and it's as if the sun is talking to me, and it's like, *Eddie, it's me, your old friend, Sun. Eddie, don't you wanna be frolicking in my glorious golden shine today? Don't you wanna feel that squishy sand between your toes? Feel that delicious slushie goodness gliding down your throat, sending that strangely pleasing shiver down your spine, the smell of hot dogs grilling, the lake waves rolling, Ava Bustamante's laughter ringing in your ears, her smile warming you up from the inside out? Anyway, I won't keep you. I just wanted to pop in and tell you how very happy I am that I get to see you today. And Beach, well, you know how much she loves having you around. She's been burying fresh seashells all week, because she knows how much you love digging around in the sand. And Lake Erie, OMG, the guy can't stop splashing around, he's so excited. Well, we'll see you soon, Eddie. Very, very soon. Hurry!*

Ohmigod, I can taste the blue raspberry syrup. I can feel the lake breeze trying to ruffle my curly hair but having no such luck, but it still feels good, you know? I can hear the little kids squealing as they chase each other down the shore. I smell the lake water, which, okay, not my favorite scent—no one's gonna bottle up Lake Erie and pass it off as cologne anytime soon, but I love it, anyway. I can practically touch the water, feel the sand clinging to my arms and chest. It's all so close. "Yes, Sun, yes, I want that. I want that so bad. There's nothing I want more," I hear myself say.

WBD's forehead wrinkles. "Huh? What is it you want, Eddie?"

"Huh? What?" I shake my head and Beach Bash fades from my mind.

"You had that creepy smiley-face thing happening. You

know, that look you get when you're up to something that's probably gon land you in trouble," The Bronster says from the couch.

I was so focused on my plan, I missed him sitting in the living room, lying in wait.

"Sorry, man, but sounds like you're staring at a mirror right now. So why don't you use it to pluck that arm-length hair fluttering from your nose and stop interrupting me and Calvin's flow, yeah?" I hit him back.

"How 'bout I pluck my nose hair when you schedule an appointment to have your lips surgically removed from Calvin's butt?"

"Whoa, guys, c'mon," WBD says, holding up both hands like he's a traffic cop. "No need to be rude. Now, Eddie, you were saying . . . ?"

"I don't know. You'll probably think it's corny," I say with a shrug.

WBD wags his head. His smile shape-shifts into a look of reassurance and understanding. "Listen, there's no such thing as corny. Especially when it comes to the things we want and need and . . . feel."

I slide my hands into my swim trunk pockets and rock on my bare heels as if I'm thinking hard on whether I should say it. This move's called dangling a worm on a fishing line. And WBD, well, let's just say he takes the bait—

"You can always tell me anything, buddy. Especially matters of the heart," WBD says, tapping his chest.

Hook, line, and sinker.

The Bronster rolls his eyes hard and snorts loud enough to make an entire pen of ugly pigs jealous—this is when I'd normally shoot him a look like, *If you blow this for me, I'll haunt you for the duration of your days on this planet* except I can't risk breaking this connection WBD and I have going right now. So as painful as it is to ignore my super-idiotic brother, I instead keep my focus locked on WBD's big, squishy heart of gold. "It's just that I . . ." I shrug. "I'd love it if we could . . . I don't know . . . use today as . . . as a way for us to get closer, you know? I get I haven't always made things easy for you, but it's not because I don't like you. I think you're pretty cool. And clearly Mom digs you, so . . . yeah, I just was hoping you and I could . . . spend some quality time, you know what I'm saying?"

"Eddie, I . . . you have no idea . . . I'm sorry." WBD pauses, attempting to regain his composure, his voice cracking a bit more with each word.

And I know what you're thinking: *Eddie, wow, isn't it kinda wrong to play with the guy's emotions?*

You're right, it's not cool at all, but hear me out, okay?

In any other situation, if by chance me and WBD were to cross paths—say I walked into seventh-grade science class this coming school year and there he is sitting behind the teacher's desk and he's all: *Good morning, I'm Mr. Eady, and you're Eddie Holloway, right? I've heard great things about you, my friend*; or suppose Mom drags me to the dentist and I'm strapped into that torture chair while some random dude jabs my teeth with a shiny, miniature spear, and I'm thinking, *Okay, what's it gonna take for Mom to knee this random dude in the gut, pull me out of this chair, and drive me to my favorite burger spot as an apology for nearly sacrificing her favorite son to the dental gods? Is faking a heart attack the move? Wait, do twelve-year-olds even have heart attacks? Other than clutching my chest and plaster- ing a look of agony on my face, what other symptoms do I gotta have to pull this fake heart attack off? Also, which side of my chest is my heart on again?* when in strolls a smiling Dr. Eady, rocking Birkenstocks with his baby-blue scrubs like, *Eddie, there he is, how's my favorite patient doing?*—we'd get along well. We'd be perfectly cool. Now, would we ever be BFFs or invite each other to basketball games and family cookouts? Well, let's see—dude's at least twenty years older than me, drinks milk that grows outta the dirt, and majorly sucks at video games. So, nah.

But I guess what I'm saying is: It's nothing personal. I don't have anything against the guy—you know, aside from the fact that he married my mom and parks his precious Betsy in the same spot in the garage where my Real Dad always parked.

"Eddie, you have no idea," he manages, his voice still cracking. "You have no idea how happy . . ." He gives up on the speech and instead takes a few steps closer to me. Holds his hand out to me for a shake. And I shake his hand with all the enthusiasm I can muster. And we stand there, in the middle of the kitchen, shaking hands for several moments past normal until finally WBD finds his singsongy voice and says, "Count me in, my friend. This is gonna be the best beach trip ever. I can feel it in my bones."

And I can't help but smile because I've done it.

I've successfully completed this leg of the mission.

WBD Beach Bash is basically a go. WBD will change Mom's mind, tell her this is a thing that has to happen, that it's the moment we've all needed, a chance to connect as a *family*, for him and me to be *pals*, *friends*, *buds*. And laundry or no laundry, there's no way Mom could say no to that. Hahaha, Eddie, you've still got it, my man. You've still got it. I can't believe you ever doubted you, hahaha.

Now for the final nudge to seal this whole deal:

"Well, I gotta say I was already pumped about today, but now that I know you and I are on the same page, I can hardly contain my excitement. Thanks for making it easy to express my feelings, Calvin."

"Oh, brother, I'mma need crackers for all this cheese? Please, just make it stop," The Bronster says, burying his face into the couch cushions to hide from the awkwardness.

But WBD is eating it up. "You don't know how good it feels to hear you say that. I know it can be hard for some men to share their emotions, but I believe it's the only way any of us can grow as humans."

"I can definitely learn a lot from you, Calvin, I see that now."

I nod as I walk across the tile to leave the kitchen, but instead I stop in the doorway, lightly slapping the wall with my right hand, keeping my back to WBD. "Oh, shoot. There is something that could ruin our whole bonding-time thing. I'm such an idiot. I can't believe I forgot . . ." I let my voice trail off, waiting for WBD to ask . . .

"What is it, man? What's up?"

I shrug as I slowly turn back to face him, that former smile of mine now all the way gone, replaced with the biggest frown my face will hold. "I don't know if I should say. I don't wanna drag you in the middle of anything, especially after we just had such a great talk."

WBD shakes his head. "Hey, hey, now, we talked about this. You can share anything with me and I'll help whatever way I can."

I bite my lip as if I'm really chewing this whole thing over. "It's just that, I sorta devised this whole summer laundry plan, it's probably the best plan I've ever come up with. And basically, tomorrow was gonna be my major laundry day. Figured I'd play hard with my family today and then work hard tomorrow, you know?"

WBD nods. "Makes perfect sense to me."

"I know, right? To me, too. Except . . ."

WBD leans in closer, even though we're on opposite sides of the kitchen now. "Except what?"

"Mom disagrees with us, which is well within her parental rights—you won't get any argument from me on that, but—"

"He's grounded until he does his laundry and so no Beach Bash for him," The Bronster chimes in, jumping off the living room couch and moving toward me. Except because he's munching on popcorn left out from yesterday evening's family movie night, it comes out more like, *He's groundkjlkl until he does khd-lafj and so no kjljch Bash for him.*

Which, whew. Let's hope WBD doesn't speak fluent Bronster.

"Umm, pretty sure no one asked for your help, thanks," I shoot back.

But The Bronster's not done. "Geez, enough with all the melodramatics, little bro. You're in our kitchen, you're not on a Broadway stage."

"I'm so sorry for wanting to spend quality time with my family, instead of driving a thousand hours to go see my girlfriend."

"It's only ninety minutes and at least I have a girlfriend to go see."

I roll my eyes. "She moved a thousand hours away from you. Are we sure *she* wants to see *you*?"

And as soon as the words leave my mouth, I already know I'm gonna get it. The Bronster tries to punch me in the shoulder, but I move out the way and he creams the wall with his fist. Of course, this only makes him angrier, and regrettably, I can't dive out of the kitchen fast enough before he's pulling me into a headlock—wedging my face between his arm and side, my nose pushed into his armpit. Honestly, I've spent a lot of my life trapped in my brother's pits, a fact I'm not proud of. I groan louder than necessary—because as far as I'm concerned, our kitchen *is* Broadway—and WBD is all over it.

Separating us from each other, he's all: "Hey, now, this is a nonviolent household, yeah? You guys are more than brothers. You're friends. One day you're gonna realize the true value of brotherhood and—"

"The only value this little weasel has is he's the perfect size to be my human footstool," The Bronster shouts, trying to reach around WBD to grab me again.

"Ha, well, at least I have value. Every time we leave you out for trash day, the garbage dump keeps sending you back."

"Okay, fellas, that's enough. I think you should both apologize to each—"

Except WBD never finishes his sentence.

"What's going on in here?" Mom says, literally appearing out of thin air. I've said it before and I'll say it again, guys—moms are the real magicians! Talk about an entrance.

"Just having a little bonding time, Mom," The Bronster says, sneering at me. "Isn't that right, Eddie?"

I nod, even though the last thing I wanna do is agree with anything that caveman says. Normally Mom would have a lot more to say, but this time she lets it go, clearly distracted as she pushes past us.

"What's going on, honey?" WBD asks.

The three of us, wedged side by side in the kitchen doorway, watch her race around the kitchen. First, she's lifting a pile of mail and then tossing it back into the little wicker basket at the end of the counter and then she's checking the kitchen table.

"Mom, what's up?" I ask.

But she's not hearing us—in fact, I'm pretty sure she's talking to herself under her breath, a thing she does whenever she's feeling stressed or nervous. Except what's she got to be worried about?

"I can't find it," she finally says, her voice muffled as she cranes her neck to search for whatever *it* is under the couch.

"What are you looking for, Mom?" The Bronster asks.

But Mom doesn't answer; she's too busy crawling on her knees to check under our two squishy living room chairs. Then she's peeking under the end tables. Then she's picking up her briefcase and riffling through its main compartment and its pockets— Mom's an *attorney*, which means she's a lawyer who represents people when they have to go to court. Except she's not just any lawyer. She specializes in environmental law and fights large companies whose factories and products pollute the environment.

Eddie, your mom is a lawyer but you still thought you could out-talk and out-argue her?

Okay, fair, guys. That's fair.

"Has anyone seen my bracelet?" Mom asks the three of us.

WBD scratches his chin. "The one Malcolm gave you?"

And all three of us look at Mom, waiting for her to answer, waiting to see *how* she'll answer.

Because two things:

1. The bracelet in question? One of my mom's most valuable

   possessions.

2. Malcolm, the guy who gave it to her? Yeah, that's my dad.

   My Real Dad.

But we never get an official answer from Mom because suddenly she's thrusting the bracelet in the air. "Found it!"

700

A few minutes later, Mom is leaning against the kitchen island, her eyes locked in on me with laser precision as she munches back-to-back strips of bacon like a human paper shredder.

Since I'm apparently an unexpected guest in Mom's dog-house now, and seeing how I'm not sure how much of me and WBD's earlier convo she might've heard, the smart play is to turn up the charm to *Wow What an Awesome Kid You Are, My Favorite Son, No Wonder You Alone Will Inherit All of My Earthly Possessions* status—even if it means pretending WBD isn't easily lapping the field for World's Corniest Stepdad Ever. Play my cards right and I escape this punishment stay-cation sooner than later. Play them wrong and, well, let's just say 100 Doghouse Lane might be my new permanent mailing address.

But there's one way all of this could go up in flames—

Because what if WBD decides to tell Mom I tried to fool him into coming to my rescue? That happens and me and my Beach Bash chances are really gonna be burnt to a crisp.

Except a few seconds later WBD says something that completely confuses me. "So, you ready for a gorgeous, fun-filled day at the beach, partner?" WBD is putting together a picnic feast for the cooler. He's stacking sandwiches six slices of twelve-grain bread high—which just seems really show-off-y, you know. I mean, I can't even name *four* grains. "Is there any better feeling than digging your toes in wet sand?"

What is this guy doing? Is he being serious right now or just trying to set me up to really stick it to me with Mom? Had I actually lucked out and he hadn't heard The Bronster say I was grounded? I shrug, thinking *welp*, until I figure out what in the world WBD is doing I guess should play along and be my normal witty self. "Being married to my mom maybe?"

The Bronster cracks up. "Good one, gerbil." And I can't tell if he's genuinely complimenting me or being his normal jerk self, but if I were forced to guess, I'd go with the latter. Also, did he just call me a gerbil?

WBD laughs, throws his hands up, including the one holding a slice of bread.

"You got me, my friend. You got me. But obviously, everything pales in comparison to being married to this beautiful human," he says, closing the distance between him and Mom and planting a really gross kiss on her cheek.

"Well, it's nice to be with someone who really knows his way around the kitchen," Mom says.

That hits me hard.

I get that she didn't actually say *my Real Dad was a terrible cook* or anything. And it's not even like I'm saying she can't compliment WBD—I mean, do you, Mom. But do me a favor? Please don't use my Dead Real Dad as a way to make your new man feel good. I haven't been able to verify this yet but I'm pretty sure WBD is crazy rich or has some insanely cool but super top secret talent, because why else would Mom be into him? Especially when not even twenty-one months ago she still had *Real Dad*.

I don't get it.

WBD and Mom giggle into each other's faces, speaking gibberish only they understand. And this is a thing I've learned: "Love" makes you look silly.

"Actually, I'm grounded, so no Beach Bash, *the* social event of the entire year, for this guy," I say, jabbing my thumb into my chest.

Pausing his popcorn devouring, The Bronster looks up long enough to cackle like a deranged hyena.

WBD backs away from Mom, frowning. "Grounded?" Except WBD says it as if he's actually hearing it right now for the very first time. He looks at Mom, then at me, then back to Mom, as if I've just said I was shooting hoops with the Easter Bunny this morning or something else wildly ridiculous. "Seriously?"

"I tried to tell you," The Bronster grumbles, bits of Pop-Tarts falling from his crusty lips.

WBD wags his head. "Aww, well, that's no good. Gee, what happened?"

Mom folds her arms across her chest. "Someone decided not to do their laundry for half a summer, that's what happened."

WBD lets loose a low whistle. "Well, that's *also* no good, comrade." But then he nods at Mom and I see that familiar do-gooder look cross his face.

"Babe," he says, his voice singsongy again. This guy is *good*. I mean, he should be nominated for an Academy Award with this acting performance. Seriously, it's that special. "Any way we can postpone his punishment until like tomorrow . . ."

Yes, WBD, do your thing!

". . . I mean, it's Beach Bash, his favorite day of the year, and we had family bonding time planned and—"

Mom clears her throat in a way that says *this is nonnegotiable* and WBD pauses. "We had a deal, didn't we, Eddie?"

"Yeah, Eddie, what about the deal?" The Bronster joins in.

I don't wanna nod but I have to. "Yes, ma'am." And I consider making one last desperate attempt at changing her mind, except she's glaring at me and WBD so hard I'm pretty sure she can see our skeletons.

"Right," Mom says. "And a deal's a deal."

And I want to argue so bad. I want to say, yes, but what about the deal you made with me, that you weren't gonna try to replace my Real Dad? Do you remember, Mom? Or are you starting to forget?

And now here we are.

WBD gives me a side glance like, *Sorry, bud, I tried, but you know your mom and her deals; this time you're going to have to live up to the bargain.*

"I'll tell you what, pal, if you get all your laundry done quickly enough today, shoot me a text and I'll come back and get you so we can have a little bit of family time together after all. How's that?"

He shoots a look over to Mom for approval.

I can tell that WBD just scored some points with her for being a kind, thoughtful, and resourceful stepdad.

She nods at him while shooting me a "be thankful for this man" expression.

I sidestep this look and reach into the cabinet directly above the stove—grabbing the see-through orange pill bottle with my full name and our address typed on its label next to the instructions to *take one pill every morning and take one pill every evening.* I pop the top, shake one pill into my palm, and gulp it down with a swig of water from the kitchen faucet.

When I turn around Mom's face has changed and she's giving me her *I'm proud of you* look. And I can't even lie—that face? Gets me every time.

800

Pause, can I be real with y'all?

In therapy last week Dr. Liz said that because of all the transitions I'm experiencing right now, I should pay closer attention to *why* I'm doing and saying. Truth? She's a cool doc but I think she worries a lot that I'm gonna spiral out of control. That maybe if I'm not careful I might undo all my hard work I've put in trying to understand how my ADHD actually affects my life and which strategies and action plans work best for me.

Which I appreciate Doc for. She's one of the only people who I feel like try to understand me, who truly listen to what I have to say, instead of just trying to tell me what I'm doing wrong—which is how a lot of adults like to roll. And I dig that Doc agrees with me—that when you start to understand the way your own mind works, when you really zero in on the ways that your brain

54

pushes you to respond versus the ways that seem to work best, well, then ADHD is no longer this ugly thing that everybody likes to roll their eyes at. Seriously, I can't tell you how many people learn about my diagnosis and start treating me like I'm some ticking time bomb, you know, instead of like an actual person who's just trying to be his best, same as anyone.

It's like my Real Dad always said, "Eddie, everything about us, everything we are inside, and all the things we feel—they're a kind of power—and that power is ultimately what you decide you want it to be. ADHD is not a weakness, Eddie. It's your superpower."

900

Do you know what it's like to watch everyone get ready for the one thing in the entirety of the universe that you're most excited for except you're not allowed to join in?

Do you know what that's like with The Bronster as your brother? Oh, no? You have no idea? Well, lucky for you, I'm willing to share my personal journey. That's right, friends, stay tuned for another thrilling episode of *SUPER MISUNDERSTOOD: THE EDDIE GORDON HOLLOWAY STORY.*

So, I'm sitting on my bed, minding my own business, totally not being hurt or affected by all the crumminess that's happened in only the first three hours of my being awake. Nope, instead I'm being Super Positive and displaying an Awesome Attitude, not even thinking about how my entire family—you know, the people whose sole job and purpose in life is to support you and make you happy—has betrayed me, treating me like a human trash can, tossing all their garbage *this is why I'm betraying you right now* excuses. My personal fave so far is one I've heard before but just can't seem to get enough of:

Hopefully this teaches you an invaluable lesson about responsibility, Eddie.

Yep, they're just lifting my lid and depositing all their crumbled-up sadness, shards of heartache, and smelly, moldy regret.

Do trash cans get sad sometimes? Sure. What do we think, because they're plastic or metal they don't have feelings? Sorry to break it to ya, but they dent and crack like all of us. But the thing that no one ever gives trash cans enough credit for is: *No matter how much garbage we throw at them, they keep showing up, they keep standing tall. Trash cans are strong, and even when we tell them they can't go to the party of the year, they . . . they . . .*

Okay, maybe I *am* in my feelings. Just a bit. A *lil* bit. Which, for anyone who knows measurements, a lil bit is basically an amount so small you need a super-high-powered microscope to even *sorta* see it.

But also, if I were *really* in my feelings, I mean buried like the way an ostrich torpedoes its head into sand, it would be completely understandable because, ummm, how would you feel if you'd literally built your entire summer vacation around one glorious day of fun in the sun, only to have everything you dreamed of, worked so hard for, planned for down to the bit-bit details, all snatched away a mere hour before the festivities began?

And for what? Oh, because you did something so unspeakably, terrifyingly awful that your mom *had no choice* but to ground you, because every parent's worst fear is raising the type of kid who grows up to be the type of adult who *gasp* skips out on laundry to hang out with their family and friends for a sunny day at the beach, right?

Wait, I didn't catch what you guys just said.

Oh, you wanted me to know ostriches don't actually bury their heads in the ground.

Gee, thanks, guys. Remind me again: Whose side are you on here? Anyway, I'm on my bed staring at my TV, which isn't even on, because I'm in shock. Because I'm trying to process what went wrong, how things nosedived so quickly.

And okay, I know you wanna say it so just spit it out already: *Eddie, instead of pouting and feeling sorry for yourself, why not just get started on that laundry? After all, the sooner you wash and dry your clothes, the sooner you'll have a slushie in your hand and wet sand between your toes.*

To which I reply: Were you trying to rhyme or was that just a happy accident?

But also, you're right. But first, you need to know two things:

1. Why the laundry doing in this house is the absolute worst!

2. The truth about basements that no one wants you to know!

1000

Let's mix it up and start with Point #2 first—

Also known as: **THE SHOCKING <u>TRUTH</u> ABOUT BASEMENTS THEY DON'T WANT YOU TO KNOW— BASEMENTS EXPOSED!!**

First of all: Think about it. All the things we love—our family and friends—we keep in safe places. All the things we prize— books, cars, clothes, jewelry, video games, art supplies, bikes, etc.—we keep in safe places.

So then, doesn't the fact that we keep our washers and dryers in the saddest, draftiest, most depressing room in the house tell us all we need to know about how unimportant laundry really is? Think about it. Take away the washer and dryer and a basement is just a miserable, crumbling concrete box.

I'm telling you, guys, laundry is a scam. A hoax. A con. Problem is, no one's talking about it. Which is why I've put together a little list I like to call:

Eddie's Unassailable Insights Into
Why Laundry Is a Scam/Hoax/Con

1. Most basements are dark, dank, and vulnerable to every sort of infestation—mice, ants, roaches, squirrels, etc. Which is why in the Middle Ages, we had another word for basements—we called them dungeons.

2. The word *basement* would make you think, *Oooh, the "base" is definitely where I wanna be!* You know, given a childhood of hide-and-seek and baseball and other things that include a home base. That would all make sense. That seems on its soapy surface to be a logical argument—except for one thing. To those familiar with Latin, the Dead Sea Codex—one of the foremost discoveries of the eighteenth century, mind you—there we learn the *true* origin for the word *basement*.

And in fact, you may be shocked to learn the word itself, as we know it, is incomplete.

The actual word found in those ancient scrolls is: *basementalgiasaghań*, which when properly translated means *base me(a)nt to be avoided*. Which I think you'll agree *changes the meaning entirely*. I mean, it's easy to see how our incorrect definition came to be—whoever was transcribing on those old flimsy scrolls was probably tired and while pouring their eighth cup of coffee lost sight of their rock mug and boom—coffee all over the scrolls. And even though they most definitely remembered to *blot* not *wipe*—it was too late. And the true meaning of *basement* was lost for centuries.

3. Basements are the very bottom of the structure. Literally *under*ground—and if a room created *under* the layer of this earth doesn't feel like an afterthought, well, I don't know what does.

4. *But, Eddie, there are laundry rooms that* aren't *in basements— what about those?* We call those aberrations—which is a

fancy way of saying, for every rule, there are exceptions. And if you are one of those rare (and super-privileged) souls who doesn't have to do their laundry in the creepy confines of a basement, well, congratulations, you are better (and safer) than the rest of us. Enjoy it! And if you are an awesome human who is the kind of person who *knows* there is more happiness in giving than in getting, consider inviting your closest friends (and their bags of laundry) over for a non-basement laundry party.

But also, even if you are that non-basement-laundry-room unicorn, you aren't completely out of the woods. Because while *location location location* is *one* of the most important ingredients for a successful laundry routine, that's merely the beginning, my friends.

Fair warning, what comes next is A LOT.

So, pause—and only turn the page when you are absolutely ready to have your whole mind blown.

1100

See, laundry in our house is not your ordinary clothes-cleaning situation.

I probably can't even explain what an *ordinary* laundry situation *is*—but were I to guess, I'm imagining for most people it goes something like:

1. Throw clothes into washer and start washer.
2. Remove clothes from washer and insert into dryer. Start dryer.
3. Fold.

THE END.

Simple, right?

Not so in the Holloway family home—no, in our house, washing and drying clothes is easily the most overly complicated, stupidly complex process ever in a house that has a ton of overly complicated, stupidly complex processes.

And who's to blame for this laborious laundry doing?

One word, three letters, three times: Mom. Mom. Mom.

Mom is the reigning champion of a game I like to call WHY ARE THERE SO MANY STEPS?

Take The Bronster, for example. He's been doing his own laundry Mom's way for five years and he *still* screws it up. And it's not just that he's shrinking his clothes, or turning his white shirts pink—which is bad enough—no, somehow he *loses entire outfits*! I'm talking the dude puts in five T-shirts, three pairs of socks, two pairs of shorts into the washer and dryer, but when he collects his clothes later, he only has three T-shirts, two pairs of socks, and one pair of shorts. Even when he's at the top of his laundry game, he still loses 30 percent of his clothes.

And you're like, *OMG, I didn't even know this was a thing that happened with laundry!*

I know, that's why I'm here to tell you the whole truth!

Okay, you're right, clearly no one's mistaking The Bronster

for a genius. I can't tell you the last time he read a book that wasn't 97 percent pictures. But you'd think he'd be a clothes-cleaning pro since he's awesome at pushing buttons. He presses mine all the time!

But nope, he's as confused as the rest of us in this house.

Think I'm exaggerating? Well, how do you explain the thirty-seven pages detailing exactly how our laundry should be done that Mom wrote, printed out, three-hole-punched, and stuck in a binder?

And she *laminated* the pages!

Mom insists the binder is just "helpful guidelines to make laundry fun and easy"—which is one of those total Parent Fibs that you can't believe they actually said out loud *without* laughing.

Anyway, I figure rather than just tell you that Mom's doing too much with all these laundry rules, I'll let you see for yourself.

Step #1: GATHER ALL YOUR SOILED CLOTHING ARTICLES.

Told you she's a lawyer.

Okay, let's see, where should I start, seeing as my entire bedroom is covered in *soiled articles*? Even my dirty clothes hamper is buried in dirty clothes.

While I *gather*, allow me to count down a few classic Parent Fibs from their Greatest Hits collection, yeah?

FIB: *Eat your broccoli if you wanna grow up to be big and strong.*

TRUTH: *I paid money for that broccoli. Plus, my parents made me eat it, so now I get to make you, and one day, if you're lucky, you can continue this terrible tradition with your kids.*

BONUS TRUTH: *Clearly, shoving broccoli stalks down your throat is not gonna grow your 4'11"-on-your-tiptoes butt into a 6'7" giant, but in Parent School, they're taught to pretend science doesn't exist. You know, except when it's YOUR homework.*

FIB: *There are no monsters under your bed, in your closet, or in that really dark corner of the basement.*

TRUTH: *Unless you count The Bronster, who likes to jump out from hiding places to scare the bejeezus out of you.*

FIB: *Any sentence that your parents start with the words: "Well, back in my day . . ."*

TRUTH: *The exact opposite of however your parent ends that sentence.*

FIB: *This thing you don't wanna do will be so much fun! You just gotta give it a chance!*

TRUTH: *Parents are so far removed from being a kid they wouldn't know REAL FUN if it wore a name tag on its shirt that said HI, MY NAME IS REAL FUN.*

And okay, speaking of fibs, not gonna lie, it's possible Mom was being honest when she said my clothes maybe, sorta do stink. But it's not because *I* stink! They've just been stewing in my closet for half the summer and it's not my fault it's hot as The Bronster's breath in there. Okay, so this completes the first phase of our gathering.

I've officially collected as many T-shirts, pants, shorts, underwear, and socks as I can hold against my chest—because the more I carry on each trip down to the basement, the less trips I have to make, right?

Except maybe I was a little too ambitious because this pile is so high I can't quite see over it as I blindly stumble out into the hallway, doing my best to keep my balance—

Even though I'm pretty sure I look like a restaurant waiter carrying a tray piled high with a lopsided stack of flapjacks (a funny word for pancakes) *and* the table where I'm supposed to deliver the flapjacks is on the other side of a frozen, slippery pond *and* instead of ice skates I'm wearing Rollerblades.

This is obviously the "fun" Mom was talking about.

"Hey, dweeb, you dropped something," The Bronster says, apparently in the hallway, although I can't actually see him because I can't see anything.

"Huh? No way, I didn't feel anything fall," I reply, trying to glance down at the floor but too afraid to lose my grip. "What did I drop?"

"Everything!" The Bronster cackles, karate-chopping the clothes pile from between my hands. All the clothes tumble onto the floor, except one exceptionally smelly *should be white but currently looks brown* sock.

That special sock clings to my lips.

If my legs weren't buried in my clothes, I'd charge The Bronster like a bull. "Hey, not cool, man," I grumble.

"You know what else isn't cool? You, dork!"

"We'll see who's the dork when I'm president of the United States and you're living in the sewer with all the other rat-people," I shoot back.

I remove my lips sock and fire it at him, but it just falls harmlessly onto the hallway floor and he laughs even harder. Before I can restock my sock ammo, it's too late—The Bronster's wings have already flapped him back into his dragon lair, his bedroom door slamming behind him. "Have fun, Laundry Loser!" he calls from inside.

If I had a magic wish-granting lamp and it only gave me *one* wish and I could wish for anything in the whole world except for more wishes . . . with zero hesitation, I'd wish I was an only child.

I stoop down to regather my clothes and catch a peek inside the partially opened bedroom door across from my room. Mom's smiling and humming a song I don't recognize as she packs her beach bag. If you would've asked me what my wish was after my Real Dad died, and I wasn't allowed to say *Bring my dad back to life*, I would've used my one wish on this—for Mom to smile again. All of us were sad, of course. But I don't know—I can't explain it, but seeing your mom cry and knowing there's nothing you can do to make things better for her, it's one of the worst things I've ever felt. But now here she is, smiling in a way that makes her whole face light up. And even though I hate to admit it, it's partly because of—

"Beep, beep," WBD says, ascending the stairs toward me. "Whoa, did your hamper projectile vomit all over the hallway or are you creating abstract art, bud?" I shrug, and for a second I think he's about to help me, but then he walks right by and slips into my parents' bathroom. I sigh, maybe feeling a little bad for myself, before WBD reemerges with a large white bag that looks like a fishing net.

I look at it quizzically. "What's this?"

"We can't properly *gather* our *soiled articles* without a laundry bag, can we?" He winks at me, and as I stand there wondering how to reply, he gets busy stuffing my laundry into the bag.

He holds the bag open for me and I join in the stuffing. My lips are about to form a *thank you, man* when Mom calls out, "Cal, can you come in here, please?"

"Yes, babe," he answers as he shovels the last handful into the net. He stands back up, hands me the bag, and with a quick smile and shoulder pat, he says, "You got this, bud," before disappearing into their room.

And all I have to say is, if WBD thinks just because he helped me bag up a few shirts, and because he helped Mom get her smile back, that I'm gonna ignore all the super-annoying things he does like buying oat milk or dancing around the house singing into spatulas, that I'm suddenly gonna forget my Real Dad ever existed, that he was the best dad ever created, well, ha, Wanna-Be's gonna be spectacularly disappointed.

1200

I'm carrying my second-to-last bag of laundry downstairs when I'm nearly spun a full 360 degrees.

Of course, it's The Bronster, his car keys dangling off his finger as he rushes toward the front door. "Watch it, Smallville!" he shouts at me as I cling to the stair railing to keep myself from rolling downhill. This is one of the many games my brother loves to play called: *Act Like Eddie's Responsible for All the Stupid Stuff I Do.* And though I hate to give him any credit, I gotta admit, he's really, really good at this game. "Mom, I'm out!" he shouts as he swings open the screen door.

"Be safe and call me when you make it!" Mom yells from somewhere downstairs.

The Bronster groans. "I'll text you instead," he says, stepping out onto our porch, before whirling back around with what appears to be a genuine smile on his face. Wait a minute, is he . . . is he smiling at me?

I resist the urge to look over my shoulder for any other possible smile recipients and for half a second I think *maybe* he's gonna say something semi-nice. "Hey, Eddie, I really hope you make it to Beach Bash, man."

OMG, he actually said something semi ni—

"Especially because I heard Tony Willis is gonna ask Ava Bustamante to be his girlfriend during the fireworks show. I'd really hate for you to miss that." And with one more wicked laugh for the road, he runs down our front walkway toward his car.

And I don't know which is worse, dealing with my laundry or living with that stone-cold gargoyle? Eh, hard to choose, but currently this laundry is feeling like the lesser of the two evils.

"Pardoooooon meeeeee, mahhhh fraaaaannn," WBD sings as he carries our large red family cooler toward our front entrance. I drop my net bag and push the door open for him. "Thaaaaank youuuuu, *mahhhh fraaaaannn,"* he bellows as he hurries down the same path The Bronster just took. And without even seeing what's in that red cooler, I already know its precise contents *and* exactly how it's packed.

Turkey-and-provolone-cheese sandwiches with super-crisp lettuce—because Mom knows my number one complaint about sandwich lettuce is *droopiness*. Wilted lettuce is sad lettuce, remember that.

Then carefully stacked atop the sandwich stack are little baggies of yummy nacho-cheese tortilla chips and next to those are several long sleeves of my favorite cookie—the one Mom always says she *didn't* buy because they're too sugary and are gonna give me bad skin, but then randomly a little mound of them will appear before me when I least expect it. You know, that good ole Mom Magic.

Sigh. Right about now I'd do almost anything to be stowed away inside that red cooler, munching on our family lunch as an unsuspecting Mom and WBD drove me for a day in beach heaven.

I swing the bulky laundry bag back over my shoulder, and as I step into the kitchen I imagine I'm the Reverse Santa Claus, about to board my stinky, *in desperate need of a good shower* reindeer posse, as we spend all of Beach Bash day coughing from my dust allergy as I slide down disgusting chimneys, leaving poorly gift-wrapped boxes filled with—*surprise, the thing you never wanted!*—fantastically smelly laundry to all the naughty, non-laundry-doing kids around the planet stuck at home while the rest of the world builds impressively tall sandcastles that glitter like gold, encircled by a moat wide enough to inner-tube around like a lazy river, except this moat's filled with an endless supply of Triple Berry Tongue Slap Your Brain Stupid Silly Super Slushie.

And, guys, how?

How is this my life?

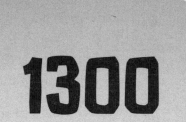

1300

Mom's flopping her butt onto our beverage cooler when I stroll past her for the basement door. I must give her a look because her face twists into challenge-mode. As in, *What, haven't you ever seen someone attempting to close something by leaping into the air and smooshing it with their butt before?*

But neither of us actually *says* anything.

I keep it moving, even throwing in a little random *sorry, I'm too busy working to stop and talk to you* whistle, because I have things to do.

And Mom keeps it flopping, because clearly, she's got water bottles to crush and soda cans to scrunch.

Had I known she was *also* watching me—which I probably should've known because moms see everything—

maybe I wouldn't have done the thing that sets her off again, but it's hard to say because honestly, it's what I *always* do. It's just that usually she's not really around to witness it.

Anyway, before you try to judge me I want you to honestly imagine what you'd do if your washer and dryer were all the way down in your cavernous basement-dungeon. If you're honest, I'm sure it's a method you'd use, too.

So, yeah, standing on the landing at the top of the stairs, I make it rain ... dirty drawers. Quickly scooping dirty sock after dirty shorts after dirty tank after dirty T-shirt, I fling all the dirty things down the beginning-to-peel gray-painted basement stairs, each bit of clothing soaring through the air for one glorious, major hang-time moment before realizing they're the equivalent of a dirty-laundry ostrich—*Eeep, we can't fly!*—and dropping like flies onto the already-in-progress huge stinky clothing heap I've created over the four previous trips.

Two reasons for this move and, no, it's not because I'm lazy, very funny, guys—

Nope. It's:

1. A mega timesaver, and in case you've forgotten, how much time this laundry takes is the only thing that matters in my life right now.
2. Fun. It's really fun shoveling your clothes downhill.

Apparently, Mom doesn't agree. How do I know this?

Because this next parental update you're about to hear is brought to you by:

SCREAM-O, the revolutionary communication tool perfected over eons and relied on by parents the globe round. Because parents, why waste precious time walking into the same room as your kid when you can just do this:

"EEEEEDDDDDDDDDDDDDDDDDD!!—DEEEEEEEEEEEEEEEEEEE EEEEEEEEEEEEEEE!!"

1400

When someone screams your name like this, it means one of two things:

1. They are seriously wounded.
2. There's a mountain lion in the house.

But if you live with my mom, it means something else.

"Mom, what's going on?" I ask, diving into the kitchen where I last saw her.

But she's not in the kitchen. The beverage cooler is there, its lid still not sealed, chunks of ice melting all around it. That poor ice, casualties of Mom's aerial booty assault. I bet they never saw her coming. I round the corner and see Mom standing in my dirty-clothes-launching spot. She's got one hand on her hip and the other is pointing down the basement stairs—and as I assumed, she is not hurt, nor is there a mountain lion on the loose.

"Boy, I *know* you're not over here *throwing* your nasty clothes down my clean stairs onto my clean floor," she says. Well, I think she *says*, although her voice also has this very distinct *asking* quality, which I gotta say is kinda a habit of hers, and a move that I still haven't quite learned how to handle.

My instincts are to spout off something clever or point out that it's because of *me* that *her* basement stairs and *her* basement floor are clean in the first place—those tasks two of the many annoyingly random chores I've been forced to do during my summer of "freedom."

I mean, what do I have to lose, right?

Umm. WRONG, guys! Majorly wrong! That was just a test to see if you'd steer me the right way and you failed miserably, sheesh. What do I have to lose? This is my mom, you've met her already, right? What I have to lose is *my whole life.*

What, you didn't know that moms are trained in the classic art of soul snatching?

Well, consider yourself lucky, and now warned, my friends.

And thanks for nearly costing me my life, too. I hook you up from the very beginning with some cool features and you hook me up with a first-class ticket to BUH-BYE!

Mom repeats herself. "Eddie Gordon Holloway, did you hear me? I asked you a question."

Ah, so it *is* a question! Confirmation received!

"No, Mom," I say as softly and as innocently as my voice will allow. "I'm not . . ."

She wags her pointing-down-the-stairs hand. "So, how do you explain all of this?"

I bat my eyes as if I'm a toddler on the first day of preschool. "I meant, no, I'm not . . . *now*. If you're asking was I *ever* throwing my nasty clothes down *our* clean stairs onto *our* clean floor, well, then, yes, I am guilty of those charges and as I stand before you, Your Honor, I beg for forgiveness and throw myself at the mercy of the court, as swiftly as my nasty clothes were thrown into the basement."

And then squeezing my eyes closed to emphasize my willingness to accept whatever punishment she considers fair, I hit her with the ace I keep hidden up my sleeve.

But, Eddie, you aren't wearing a shirt.

It's a figure of speech, guys.

Okay, so what's the ace, then?

Oh, nothing much—just my patented, super-special, never-fail countermove to Mom's possible soul-snatching attack. Yep, it's a look I call: SURPCERN.

And you're like, "Wait, *surpcern*, Eddie? C'mon, man, that sounds like an energy drink."

Trust me, surpcern is waaay more beneficial to your health—especially if we're assuming you'd like to live deep into your teenage years.

Okay, okay, you have our attention, what is surpcern, Eddie?

Well, I'm glad you asked. SURPCERN is THEE single most important expression that you absolutely, unequivocally MUST MASTER should you wish to not only survive your tween years, but dare I say, *emerge victorious* from those same years.

Surpcern is when you make your face look both *SURPrised* and *conCERNed* AT THE SAME TIME.

As in, *Oh wow, I'm so surprised this thing is happening to you, especially when it's related to something you asked me to do that either I failed to do entirely or, per your standards, did not do sufficiently.*

The concern is where you really earn your money, though. This is how you assure your parental figure that it is THEIR health and best interests that are most important to you. That you hate to see them like this: afraid, or sad, or angry, or hurt.

No question, surpcern is *the* premier facial expression for all kid-parent occasions. Never leave home without it.

When I finally reopen my eyes I see Mom's eyes are clenched closed—and now I'm worried. Because this is her *Child, you're giving me a headache* face. "Eddie, you didn't want to walk down the stairs like you've got some sense?"

To which I wanna reply: *Umm, is this a trick question?* But instead, I say, "What's the difference how the clothes get downstairs as long as they make it there?" And no, I don't ask this question to be smart or funny—but because I genuinely don't understand the problem here.

She's massaging the top corners of her face now, trying to ward off that headache, which appears to be coming in red hot. "The difference is this is a mess, Eddie. You don't see that?"

I make a show of peering down the stairs at my clothes pile. "I see that pile, yes. But, Mom, I gotta say, respectfully, if I'm gonna just toss them in the washer machine in a few minutes, who cares if they sit on the basement floor—"

"On *my* clean basement floor."

And okay, honestly, guys, this whole insistence on the basement floor being somehow clean is baffling. Because while it is not dirty, no one is gonna prepare a meal and then eat that meal directly on the basement floor, even immediately after I've cleaned it, soooo—

And I should say this, because in fairness to Mom, while she's always run a tight ship, she's been kind of especially moody this last week. Were I to guess why, I'd say it's because she feels weird about Beach Bash.

Other than their small wedding (there were like twenty people invited) and a few trips to the grocery store, Mom hasn't really been anywhere super public with WBD. Which means this is kinda the first time our neighbors and friends see her not only minus my Real Dad—

But *with* WBD.

So, yeah, I can imagine she's a little nervous.

Anxious about how things might play out today.

What if people judge her for marrying someone else not even

two years after Dad died? Or what if they hate WBD and so then they start hating Mom by association?

And I understand why people might feel a kind of way about the situation, because honestly, I do, too.

"Babe, you ready to take off? Where are you at?" WBD calls from the other side of the house. And Mom gives me a look like she's deciding whether or not she's done with our conversation, but in the end, it's me who speaks first.

"Have fun, Mom," I tell her. And I mostly really mean it.

1500

WBD takes one last long look at me, gently wagging his head with what I can only guess is deep regret—as he drags our front door closed behind him and Mom. But then he pauses and meets my eyes, cuffing his hands around his lips like he's about to tell me a secret. "The washing machine?"

"Yeah?" I say.

His hands are still shielding his mouth even though Mom is already down the driveway, standing next to her car—they always take her car, never his super-special ride collecting dust under a protective covering in the garage—and leans toward me. "There's a Quick Wash cycle for a reason." He winks at me. "See you sooner than later, tiger." And then the door's clicking shut and he's gone.

I dive onto the living room sofa and peek out the big window.

"Oh, shoot," I say, immediately ducking back down as WBD, in his way-too-short bright blue shorts and way-too-skinny aloha shirt, pats his pants pockets as if he's forgotten something, before swinging back toward the house, his eyes aimed right at me.

I'm not entirely sure *why* I duck. It's not like I'm doing anything wrong. Basically, I'm watching my mom abandon me—what happened to *no kid left behind??*—for the party of the year and the girl of my dreams. *And* if you think about it, *they're* the ones who should be ducking from *me*, who should be embarrassed to meet *my* eyes, because if anything they're doing me—Mom's *only* chance at having non-mutant grandkids one day—so wrong. I mean, one day she's gonna need me to take care of her. Seriously, I feel like this is something parents don't think about enough. Which is weird because Mom is always going on and on about *doing everything I can to make sure I have a bright future*. Ha, maybe it's *her* future she should be worried about.

I hear Mom call out, "Your keys are already in the car, babe. Remember, you wanted to cool it down before we left?" I inch back up toward the window and watch WBD laugh, heading back toward the car while Mom attempts to load her famous banana pudding into the back seat without it tipping over—

Which, *ahem*, wouldn't even be an issue if I were in the car where I belong—because that's my job. I am the Protector of Pudding (and All Other Transported Perishable and Extremely Spillable Goods). It's a responsibility I don't take lightly, whether it's peach cobbler, or a pan of lasagna, or a ginormous bowl of sloshing soup—which, let me tell you, is no picnic! Ha! Get it? No pic—

You know what, forget it. Point is—

No one wants the back seat smelling like rotten bananas because the lid popped off on the ride over, least of all the human who always sits back there.

Which is to say the Points of the Actual Point is:

I should be on my way to Beach Bash, *and* ugh, adults are the worst.

1600

Let's officially add everything about this morning to the Things Adults/Parents Don't Understand list:

When you're a kid, you don't get a lot of say in what happens in your day-to-day life. No, adults are deciding, or have already decided, pretty much ALL OF YOUR ENTIRE LIFE from the TIME YOU ARE BORN through, at the very least, your EIGHTEENTH BIRTHDAY!

You *have* to eat your vegetables before you can leave the table.

You *have* to get all your shots so you can go to school.

You *have* to go to school.

You *have* to go to the party for the kid who doesn't even like you.

You *have* to invite that kid to your party and tell them *thanks for coming* with a stupid smile on your face, while your mom looks on.

You have to wear the outfit that you absolutely hate even though they know that it makes you look ugly, nerdy, huge, weird, like a stick insect, like a wombat, like a baby possum.

You *have* to do your chores, or risk punishment.

You *have* to do your chores *exactly* how they say, or risk more punishment.

You *have* to go to bed even though you're not even slightly tired, and yes, right now, head upstairs, and I don't wanna hear any complaining, either, you know what your bedtime is. And no, I don't care if you're wide awake, you don't have to go to sleep, just get in bed and close your eyes and don't move or make any noise for a minimum of eight hours, okay? Wait, no kiss good night?

I mean, are you kidding me? What gives them the right, you know? And don't say, *Well, Eddie, they gave birth to you. They created you.* Because let's be real, literally every human ever was made by someone. Big flipping whoop. Who even cares about something that happens to *everyone*?

1700

At this point, I'm not gonna lie to you—it's a lot of dirty laundry. A LOT.

Like I still stick by my plan because it's not only thoughtful, it's pretty next level—you know, if it had been allowed to continue (shout-out to The Breaker of Great Plans who more times than not I just call Mom).

Naturally, I stuff as much laundry into the washer as humanly possible, completely ignoring Mom's voice in my head warning me of the danger—*Eddie, don't overfill the washer machine unless you want it to explode and turn the basement into a swimming pool*—because sorry, Mom, but (1) finishing quickly is worth *any* risk and (2) uhh, yes, I'd love an indoor all-seasons pool, are you kidding me? I mean, we live in Ohio—otherwise known as the Buckeye State, the Heartland, and The Place

Where It's Exceptionally Cold 9.5 Months Out of 12! A heated indoor pool? Umm, sign me up!

I press a few buttons, like Mom taught me, and I turn the selector dial to NORMAL load, which is weird, let me just say, because (1) how do they expect you to know if your load is "normal"? and (2) how does that make all the other loads feel when they're categorized as non-normal? Like has anyone thought of that? I mean, it's bad enough we're separating clothes by colors but now we're judging their normalcy? That's what's not normal, you ask me. But whatevs.

I flip Mom's laundry binder manual to the next page.

Centered, underlined, and in bold type at the top of the page is one word:

<u>DETERGENT</u>

And you're like, *Wait, Eddie, is there really an entire section devoted to detergent?*

Again, have you met my mom? Of course there is. She leaves nothing to chance.

It says, first locate the bottle of detergent.

Sounds easy enough.

I know for a fact that Mom keeps the detergent in the cabinet above the basement sink. I open the cabinet and immediately my face falls.

Because there's not a single bottle of detergent inside.

No, there are a *half dozen* different bottles of detergent of different shapes, sizes, and colors. A quick glance at their labels and yep, they even have different scents: Pine Fresh, Rainy Spring Day, Cinnamon Toast with Butter—

Okay, I made that last one up but you see my point. How in the world am I supposed to know *which* bottle is the right bottle for *which* type of laundry?

And I know what you're thinking: *Eddie, the binder!*

Which would make sense, because it shows how to measure the amount you need for the size of wash you're loading, and where to pour the detergent, but what it absolutely does not say anywhere among the thirty-seven whole pages is:

WHICH BOTTLE?!

And so I ask you, how in the world do you write thirty-seven detailed pages about how to do laundry without specifying the main laundry-doing ingredient?!

I pull my phone out and fire off a text to her.

EDDIE (to MOM): Hey, which laundry detergent do I use?

I wait for my message to say *delivered* like it always does but nothing happens. I can't even tell if it's been sent. Maybe they're in a bad reception area or something. In my head, I attempt to visualize the route we take to the beach, trying to imagine where they might be where the cell service is terrible. But my brain isn't cooperating and I can't think past the first quarter of the trip.

My eyes fall back on the shelf filled with detergent. Let's see, maybe there's a clue on the labels. Like a hint that'll point us in the right direction.

Bottle #1: Clean and Fresh! New and Improved Detergent Flow!

Hmm, "Clean and Fresh," I definitely like the sound of that. "New" not so much because new is not always better. But speaking of better, the "and Improved" part is a definite plus.

Bottle #2: Fresh and Clean Feel! Improved with Our Best Formula Yet!

Okay, so this is also "Fresh and Clean," except it's specifically referring to the "Feel." What's clean and fresh about Bottle #1, then? And what does "Feel" mean? Like it *feels* fresh and clean but isn't? Or more like *you're* gonna *feel* fresh and clean putting these clothes on when you're finished? Also, this one says "Improved," too. But it adds "Best Formula Yet," which sounds dope. But is it their best formula because their other formulas stunk? Or are they saying, hey you thought we were good before, check out how amazing we are now?

I check the other bottles and my fears are confirmed.

They all say pretty much the same thing.

But wait, maybe that's good? Because I can't really go wrong, then, no matter which one I choose, yeah? There you go, Eddie. Now you're thinking, ha!

But then I look to the right of the detergent and I realize I'm not even close to a decision. Because the detergent is just the start of the laundry doing.

There's also bleach—which I don't know about you but that sounds like *blood* and *leeches* to me, as in those gross slug things that stick to your skin and suck your blood. I nearly drop the bottle, I'm so disgusted. Who would name something *bleach* of all words? The only way it's ever okay to call something *bleach* is if it's the name of the person who invented the stuff.

Gloria Bleach

Troy Sanderson-Bleach IV

Otherwise, it's a nah on the bleach. Plus, I know The Bronster accidentally splashed bleach on his favorite pair of jeans and he was screaming as if he were stuck in the worst nightmare of his life—all because the bleach "ruined" his jeans with yellow-white streaks. A chemical reaction, WBD said, as if understanding that this was science would make The Bronster feel better.

Wait, but bleach isn't even the end. There's . . . fabric softener?

Seriously?

Is this really a thing?

Why do we need our clothes softened? Is cotton not comfortable enough for you people? What are you trying to do, make your shirt feel like lotion or something?

I pass on the softener, too.

After double-checking Mom's manual, I'm finally ready to get this first load going. I smile as I mash the start button and the washer machine rumbles to life—and judging from the fact that it's shaking hard enough to jackhammer through the floor, it's possible I did overfill it just a touch. It's a front-loading machine, and it has one of those round windows like you see on a ship—a port window—so it's kinda cool to see the clothes sloshing around in there as water pours into the cavity from all sides as if my dirty socks are a captured hero who's been thrown into a pit that the villain means to be their watery grave—

I'm sorry, was that too dark? See what being in the basement does? And it's only been like five minutes!

I check the washer machine because this fancy model gives you a time estimate.

One hour and fifteen minutes?!

No way.

By my calculations I have at least four loads to get through—meaning altogether this is gonna take . . . five hours?!

What?!

No way. Nope.

Beach Bash will be more than half over by then. I'll miss everything. Clearly, that's not an option. So what, then? *Think, Eddie, think.*

I study the washer machine settings more carefully until bingo, my eyes light up as I reset the machine.

This time, I press QUICK WASH, like WBD suggested.

My joy returns as seventy-five is replaced with twenty-eight minutes, reducing my TWT (total washing time) to two hours.

This still sucks because the beach is definitely calling my name, but it sucks less—three hours less to be exact.

I'm not sure who designed this particular washing machine, or if quick wash is an option on every machine, but what I do know is every now and then—when you need it the most—a little good luck rains down on you like a giant washing machine in the sky—soaking you in optimism, renewing your faith in the world. Even Life knows sometimes you need to catch a break. And okay, thanks, WBD, too, for the tip or whatever.

And so with a *things are looking up* smile on my face, I climb the two flights of stairs back to my bedroom, cannonball onto my bed, and grab my controller.

With a single button tap, *boom*—I'm back in the skies where I belong, once again an unstoppable dragon force breathing justice onto the earth one mouthful of fire at a time.

Maybe ten or fifteen minutes later, I swear I hear the washer machine's "cycle complete" chime and race into the basement only to learn it was the video game.

Why do all *beeps* sound the same? I feel like the people

who make phones, computers, video game systems, washers, and dryers would understand how important it is that all of their very different products have super-different *beep* alerts. But apparently, when they all got together at the Electronics Convention to discuss their inventions, everyone was like, *Wait, how come your beep sounds like my beep? You gotta change your beep, bro. No, no, you gotta change YOUR beep, my friend. Ha, all of you people are gonna change your beeps because I called dibs first!*

And thinking they were all smarter than the rest of them, they promised to go back to their labs and change the sound, that it was only fair that no one gets to use that special *beep*.

But they were all lying because they all kept it.

And so now I can't even listen for my laundry's *beep* without wondering if it's the microwave telling me it's finished warming up a dish, or the sound of my video game saving, or a text coming through on my phone.

And don't even get me started on TV shows, movies, and commercials these days.

They use the same beeps and chimes as our real devices.

It's wild!

Seriously, one time a phone commercial came on and I thought I had like fifteen texts but it was the guy in the ad.

There's a full twenty minutes still to go flashing on the red LED display screen, so I use that time to eat a yogurt and a handful of cashews, before slipping outside and down the driveway for the mail.

1800

Is there anything worse than when you're walking along, minding your own business, but then out of nowhere—*Crash! Bang! Boom!*—you're viciously assaulted?

But who's doing the assaulting, Eddie, and why?

It's easier if I tell you who's *not* doing it.

Nope, your attacker is *not* that attention-seeking bully from school. You know, the kid whose awful behavior is constantly glossed over by adults—your stepdad included—as a kid who's only stealing your lunch money, stuffing you into lockers, and calling you Edie because the truth is they're lonely and desperate for a friend?

Because yes, nothing says *Let's be eternal besties* more than theft. I mean, I get loneliness sucks but that's what TikTok's for, no?

And no, the attack's not even orchestrated by The Bronster—or as he's more commonly known as: *The Officially Recognized Worst Human Being Ever to Breathe on This Planet and Likely Any Other Planet with Yet-to-Be-Discovered Alien Life Forms.*

Okay, I see now that nickname could stand to be a shade shorter and, sure, while we're at it, maybe a tad less harsh. But to be fair, it's also completely accurate. Hey, not my fault the truth hurts.

Umm, Eddie, not to be pushy but we're wondering if you could maybe just tell us who the assailant actually is, you know, if that's cool?

No worries, my friends—we're gonna get there, we're almost there. The thing is we're always so much in a hurry to get to the point, to get to the thing, to get to the potty—

Like I get it, but also there's something to be said for taking your time, for taking the scenic route, for taking chances.

Anyway, so you're minding your own business, yada yada yada. You're opening the mailbox to check for your long-awaited, heavily delayed game *Heroes & Heart VI* even though who are you kidding, you already know it's not there because the Universe basically hates you today—

Or if it's not outright hatred, it's at the minimum the Universe being so bored that it said to itself: *You know what, self? Let's turn up the spice level today, yeah? Let's make this a Saturday to remember except, you know, for all the wrong reasons, hahaha.*

To which the Universe replied to itself: *Excellent idea, Universe. You know how much I love to frustrate humans. Shall I spin the Wheel of Annoyance, then?*

The Universe Itself *clapping excitedly*: *I was hoping you'd say that. Gosh, we haven't used the Wheel of Annoyance in at least what, thirty or forty . . .*

The Universe: *It's been easily a solid forty seconds. Which is thirty-nine seconds too long, if you ask me.*

The Universe Itself: *Oh, so now you're all into it, huh? Where was all that enthusiasm this morning, that's what I wanna know. The only reason you were on time for work this morning is because . . .*

The Universe (rolling its eyes): *Okay, here we go again. Tell me something: How many times must I apologize to you before you'll be ready to move on?*

The Universe Itself: *First you tell me why come every morning I've gotta literally hire an entire middle school marching band to* come and play terribly enough to force you outta your bed and into the shower?

The Universe: *Oh, I'm sorry I'm inconveniencing you, my friend. But maybe I'd have an easier time getting up if, oh, I don't know, maybe if someone didn't snore loud enough to literally rattle my bed every stinking night, maybe I'd be well rested for a change.*

The Universe Itself: *Can we agree that you're kinda exaggerating about my snoring levels?*

The Universe (shaking its head adamantly): *Umm, do you wanna listen to the recording from last week again?*

A long pause . . .

The Universe Itself: *Listen, I'm sorry, okay? You know I hate it when we fight.*

The Universe (nodding its agreement): *Me too. And I'm sorry for being so extra all the time.*

The Universe Itself: *Hey, you're not any more extra than I am, so . . . Hey, I know what'll make us feel better.*

The Universe: *Please tell me we're gonna spin the Wheel of All Human Names, too!*

The Universe Itself (chuckling): *Yep. Now go ahead and give it one of those good strong spins of yours.*

The Universe: *Say, is it bad that I'm really hoping it lands on Deny Someone the Thing They Want Most in Life?*

The Universe Itself: *Ohmigod, will you please stop reading my mind! I'll be honest, I really hope the Wheel of Human Targets lands on an Eddie.*

The Universe: *Ha, saaame. I don't know what it is about humans named Eddie that makes them so much fun to annoy, but by gosh, it's like chicken noodle soup for my soul.*

To be fair, it could easily be none of the above and just that the Universe woke up grumpy, was tossing and turning all night because it put itself out there to the Galaxy, opening up about its true feelings, and the Galaxy has yet to text back or whatever.

~~~

But back to the assault.

I'm strutting to our mailbox crazy frustrated that I'm spending my day in a basement instead of the beach. I'm hearing buzzes in my video game that make me think my laundry is done. All the while, my terrible, horrible, "lounge around the house in his underwear" brother gets to hang out with his *way too good for him* girlfriend.

That's when I hear a low "woof woof woof."

Now I know that can't be on the TV because I'm outside.

I turn around, a big smile on my face.

"Hey, boy. Hi, Mr. Bubbles."

Mr. Bubbles is sort of the shared neighborhood dog, although if any of us had our way, Mr. Bubbles wouldn't be spending so much time out living in the streets. It's true that every one of us has attempted to "adopt him" into our families, but no matter what, each time Mr. Bubbles "escapes," disappearing from the neighborhood for a day or two before running his tail-wagging self right back into all our lives.

Everyone on our block feeds Mr. Bubbles—leaving whatever it is they think dogs like, or at least what they think is best for his growth and development.

I'm pretty sure Mr. Bubbles is scoring twice as much food as he'd be fed were he living with one family full-time. Which is to say, Mr. Bubbles's refusal to commit to anyone, it's pretty much genius.

But it also means he's a big dog. And that's when Mr. Bubbles takes his cue to jump right into my legs.

I go down hard. Like flip-flops-flying-in-the-air, pile-of-human-on-the-grass hard.

To be real, I've never seen Mr. Bubbles make contact with someone. Not even when you take him to the park and he starts chasing the ducks everywhere and they let him get close enough to nudge them. He doesn't.

So it's easy to understand why when Mr. Bubbles suddenly launches into me that I'm feeling a kind of way about being outside.

What's freaking him out so bad? I wonder.

I'm still lying on my back when I look up to the sky.

That's when I notice that the real culprit of the earlier mentioned assault is not the giant dog that took my legs out. No. It's much worse.

It's the *worst luck of all time* that clobbered me.

1900

Someone set off enough fireworks to blanket not just Carterville the city, but all of Carterville County, too.

The distinct whistle of fireworks whizz through the bright blue sky—followed by *bang pop pop crackle bang crackle* as each explodes into vibrant electric eruptions.

The fireworks show is hands-down my favorite Beach Bash tradition.

Except it's barely eleven in the morning yet.

Fireworks aren't set off until nine at night.

And I know what you're thinking—*Eddie, I'm sure there's some other reasonable explanation for this. Probably some teenagers snuck away to an isolated part of the beach to let off some fireworks of their own.*

Which, fair. Every year people use the Bash as an excuse to produce their own light show.

Except shooting fireworks off during the day is just a waste of fireworks. The whole point is watching them explode against a dark sky.

Something about the way these look makes me uneasy. First Mr. Bubbles is acting weird and now this.

This feeling makes me retreat back into the house. But I'm too curious about what's happening out there to leave it alone. I need to get a better look.

I check the layout of our house to find the best spot for the view.

Essentially the Holloway house has two main living floors—

Our first floor is what Mom calls our entertaining space. You come through our front door into a short hallway that leads you directly into our kitchen and dining room and family room. "Open-floor-plan living!" is what the brochure said when we moved into this place. It's a feature that everyone loves except The Bronster, of course! He hates it.

THE BRONSTER: *It's awful—you can see our entire house from the kitchen.*

MOM: *What's so awful about that? That means we're always together.*

THE BRONSTER*: Well, what if I'm lying on the sofa in my underwear?*

MOM: *Yeah, maybe don't do that.*

THE BRONSTER: *Umm, don't do that? If I can't lie around the living room in my underwear, what's the point of even having a house?*

And although GUY CODE dictates that I have The Bronster's back in most arguments, he's on his own for this one.

Anyway, that's our first floor—entrance, kitchen, dining room, family room, and Mom's office. Pretty basic stuff.

Upstairs are three bedrooms—me, the 'rents, and (unfortunately) The Bronster—plus two bathrooms. And yes, it majorly sucks to share a bathroom with The Bronster. Don't even get me started because that's a whole story—but okay, since you're thinking about it, let me just say no matter how bad you've gotta go, do not, I repeat, DO NOT use our bathroom between the hours of nine p.m. and eleven p.m. Unless you happen to own a nuclear-level gas mask. Why, you ask?

Because The Bronster squats the bowl every day at the same time. He enters the bathroom between 8:59 p.m. and 9:03 p.m.

and exits approximately ninety minutes later. You can set your watch to it.

But you're like, *Okay but wait, you said avoid the bathroom for TWO hours but that's only an hour and a half, what gives?*—to which I say, bravo on those math skills and trust me—after The Bronster has been at work in there, the air toxicity levels are lethal for at least another thirty minutes. Honestly, were I you? I'd tack on another thirty minutes because there are some things you can't unsmell.

I decide the best place to get a better look is on the second floor, so I hit the stairs, scampering up to where our bedrooms all sit. But my bedroom's not an option since it's on the back of the house. And while Mom doesn't like me hanging out in her room when she's not around, I don't even consider creeping into The Bronster's room. If Mom catches me in her room, it's probably just a long boring lecture. But if The Bronster finds me even lurking in close proximity to his bedroom door it's gonna be World War III.

Soooo . . . Mom's room it is.

I grab binoculars from under my bed and head in there.

I guess I underestimated how weird it is to be in here know-ing that the bed Mom and my Real Dad once shared is probably rotting away in some garbage scrap heap—meanwhile, this super-ginormous fancy new bed that WBD and Mom picked out together as a way to *memorialize our fresh start together* is an annoying reminder that my Real Dad isn't just gone for a little while. And that WBD is very much here.

I can't help but think if you're the one moving into someone else's house, the same house the coolest man I've ever known and will probably ever know lived and laughed and loved, the same house where we were doing just fine because this house is already chock-full of memories, because no matter how many family pictures you help Mom take down or move into the basement, the fact remains *this is not your house.* You can move in all your stuff and rearrange every cabinet, every drawer, every shelf—but that won't change the thing we all know and feel—

You are a visitor here, my dude. This will never be your home.

I skirt by the huge bed, avoiding any contact with it, and head to the large bedroom windows that take up one wall of the room.

I climb outside onto the small second-floor balcony shared between this room and The Bronster's. There isn't any balcony on my side of the house. There's only a view of woods, woods, and more woods.

I scan the sky with my binoculars. I'd forgotten how awesome these things really are. I can see all the way out to the exact launching point for all the fireworks. I smile as the colorful aerial eruptions intensify. I gotta say the Beach Bash planning committee really went all out on the light show this year, sheesh. I can only imagine what this would've looked like at night. What a waste . . .

. . . except wait, the launch point doesn't make sense. There's no way these are being set off from the beach. No, these are erupting maybe a mile past the beach, out on the water.

I scan the waves thinking maybe there's a ship out there, or at least some boat—which doesn't seem like the safest way to light this many rockets and flares, but what do I know?

A thorough scan of the horizon and waves confirms the fireworks are *not* being triggered from anything out on the sea. In fact, stranger still—I can't find one sailboat, one ship, not even a Sea-Doo skipping across the lake.

Which would make sense if there were thunderstorms brewing.

But today it's 82 degrees with not a single cloud in the sky.

Still, there's nothing out there as far as I can see.

2000

Of course none of what I just said makes a lick of sense. You can't ever see the people on the beach from this angle, it's too far.

And it's gotta be just a coincidence that there aren't any crafts out on the water. I probably checked right at the time when everyone was docked for the dance party.

It's clear what's really happening here:

My brain is so messed up over not being at Beach Bash right now, it's playing tricks on me. I've just got too many things on my mind and my brain's struggling to keep up with the work-load. After all, it was only a few minutes ago that I rushed down into the basement, 100 percent confident I'd heard the washer machine chime, only to find the machine still swish-ing and swooshing a couple dozen pairs of my dirty drawers and just as many T-shirts.

I'm not sure if there's a medical condition for what I'm experiencing right now—but I'm pretty sure FOMO works. I mean, c'mon, really, Eddie? Thank goodness no one else is around, ha—first lucky break all day.

I check the clock on Mom's bedside table and see that my laundry should be done for real now, so I race down the stairs and back into the basement.

My first load complete, I'm transferring my clean but very wet clothes into the dryer when an important life question pops into my brain: Is there anything wetter in the entire world, water aside, than wet jeans?

Think about it. Wet jeans? Basically a lethal weapon.

You ever grab a big armful of wet clothes out of the washer and it soaks your whole shirt? Well, it's even worse when you're not wearing a shirt. Some of the water drips down below my waist but that doesn't matter—I'm in a bathing suit.

It takes a couple of tries to get everything from one machine to the other, and yes, there are a few dropped socks along the way.

The socks pick up dust bunnies from the concrete floor like a magnet.

I double-check Mom's laundry guide, and yep, it's just as I thought.

Do not forget the dryer sheet. This is a common but costly mistake.

Don't forget the dryer sheet? Duh, who'd forget dryer sheets?

Ha, here's what I don't get—we give so much credit to washers and dryers, but really *we're* doing all the work. Tossing in all the clothes, pouring in detergent, choosing the right settings, making sure all the stains are out before throwing all those wet clothes into the dryer, adding *dryer sheets* because heaven forbid the dryer actually does its *one* job *alone* . . .

I shake my head. *Dude, you're losing it. Don't let this laundry defeat you. Stay strong.*

I start the dryer. Then, oops, I remember the sheets, stop the dryer, and toss a few in because surprise—Mom's rule book doesn't specify *how many* sheets. I restart the dryer and mentally pat myself on the back like, *Way to hang in there, Eddie. Way to mount a comeback.*

And then I reread Mom's guidebook and realize it *did* specify the dryer sheets.

It said *sheet.* As in singular. As in one. As in *not a few.*

I shrug, guess that load's gonna be extra . . . I check the box for the scent . . . *new and improved "clean laundry smell."* Really?

Which *scientist* came up with that, huh? I'd love to ask them how they engineered a dryer sheet to smell like "clean laundry"? So, you're telling me the dryer sheet will not only remove the static electricity from my clean laundry, but it will also make my clean laundry smell like . . . like . . . clean laundry?

Seriously, dude?

That's dumber than that "new car" scent thingie The Bronster's got hanging from his car rearview mirror. Hate to break it to ya, but no one's hopping into that car and saying to themselves, *Ahh, the scent in here is perfect. Just like a brand-new automobile.*

I let myself laugh a little, you know, to hold back the tears because now I'm right back where I started, standing at the base of Nasty Clothes Mountain to collect another load for the washing machine. I dump the next armful in and slam the lid. I select Quick Wash, feeling a surge of happy flow through my body as I press start and the machine chugs to life. I'm not ashamed to say I'm still feeling pretty proud of that laundry hack. I stand back in front of the little window and check out the view again when it all starts.

Or, I suppose more accurately that's when things come to a complete stop.

The dryer goes dead, sending all the clothes inside ricocheting off each other.

The washing machine clicks off and the water stops rushing in.

And on top of that, the lights suddenly go dark.

Standing in the depths of our pitch-black basement, yeah, I'm definitely getting *Okay, this is bad, this is really bad, I'm gonna die, no, I'm not just gonna die, I'm gonna die alone in my creepy basement surrounded by dirty clothes and stupid laundry sheets* vibes.

Don't judge me. I already told you, I hate basements. Most of all, *so dark you can't see anything* basements.

I tap the power button on the washer machine even though I already know it's not gonna work because, duh, power's out, but you gotta rule out the stupid stuff first, you know?

Clearly we're dealing with a tripped breaker or something and the breaker box is down here, so I'm good.

I check my phone—47 percent charged. Okay, it's on the wrong side of the halfway mark but it's not terrible. I switch the flashlight app on and head to the opposite corner of the basement, feeling my way along the walls.

Of course, this isn't my first outage—there's been a few times, usually triggered by a bad storm, where the lights are suddenly flickering and then, boom, just like that, every plugged-in thing—dishwasher, TV, fridge, the hot water heater, came to a grinding halt. And then Real Dad and I would trudge downstairs into the far back corner of the basement, where apparently the power box hangs out.

Real Dad would open the box, scan the rows of switches, find the problem child and flip it back on, issue solved and then we'd march back upstairs to the living room like the heroes we were. I'd say, "The heroes have returned and we have returned light upon this land," or something equally cheesy, and The Bronster would make fun of me. Except I didn't care what he said or thought because I knew I had provided a vital service: I was the Holder of the Flashlight, or more accurately, the Holder of the Phone with Its Flashlight App Turned On—and, yeah, okay, occasionally I got a little distracted, prompting Real Dad to say,

"Eddie, sorry to bother you and your shadow puppetry, but would you mind aiming some of that light at the power box so I can, you know, see what I'm doing and not get electrocuted?"— but that was the exception, not the standard!

Now I'm bumping into storage bins stuffed with our winter clothes. I'm tripping over Mom's old bowling ball. And I nearly wipe out when I tip over a jar of golf balls. Who keeps a jar of golf balls? And yeah, I feel extra abandoned down here. And, yeah, this is officially my worst nightmare, glad you could be here. I feel something crawl across the back of my neck and I scream and almost faint—before realizing it's just a ball of yarn sticking out of a box. Except then I hear something crinkling on the ground next to me and I whirl around to escape, knocking over what I think is an old ironing board. The crinkling thing? Turns out to be a plastic bag filled with gift wrap tissue paper. If you get a present from my mom, I 100 percent promise you the paper it's wrapped in, and the tissue paper stuffed inside the decorative bag, oh, and the decorative bag—all of it's from a gift someone gave her that she's saved and reused.

It's okay, Eddie, calm down. You're not dead . . . yet.

I make my way over to the power box and pop it open. There

are rows of switches. The whole house's power right here in this box. I shine the light to the little grid that lists which switch is for which room. *Basement.* I flick it.

Nothing.

I try it again.

Nope.

So I do the only thing I can think of.

I flip them all like when you're in an elevator and you hit every button.

No lights. No sound of the dryer starting back up.

The only thing I hear? My heart thumping against my ribs.

And the only thing I feel? A sharp, hot sensation prickling under my skin, shooting up from my knees into my back and my neck—

A feeling more commonly known as *scared out of my stupid mind.*

And, yeah, all that *it's cool, Eddie, you're not dead yet* stuff, that was dumb. I take it all back.

Because I'm absolutely, positively gonna die down here. Amid boxes of junk and mildew and . . . dryer sheets. Maybe it'll be from some ugly basement creature who's been waiting for a moment like this to devour me. Or you know, maybe I'll just die from fear. Either way, I'm 100 percent, without question, no doubt about it, gonna die...in my basement... alone...doing laundry...on what should've been The Best Day of My Young Life.

2100

I'll be honest, there were times when it was a little aggravating to have someone who claimed to know *everything* and then actually seemed to know *everything*. But it's not Dad's fault he was naturally good at everything, that he always knew how to fix anything, that he always made even the worst of times so much better. Just like it's not Dad's fault that his body started acting weird and he stopped feeling so good and started spending more time at the hospital than with us.

Because sometimes things just happen that are completely beyond our control and sometimes these things really, really suck so bad, like unbelievably bad—but no matter what, nothing can take away the good times, the good memories, the good vibes.

That's what Dad told me before he closed his eyes.

See, I told you he always knew what to do.

2200

Don't judge me on this, but when I finally realize that I'm stuck in a fully-dark-basement-with-no-hope-of-light, I know there's only one way out.

Run!

I aim for where the stairs should be, then take them two steps at a time. All the way up to the top but I don't stop there.

Shooting out of the basement door, I wrap around to the other side of the house and take the next flight up to the second floor. I'm like a kid on fire. No, I'm like if you were at a bonfire roasting marshmallows over the flames, except suddenly the marshmallow jumps off your stick and starts booking it across the lawn for its ooey-gooey life!

I spend the next few minutes roaming from room to room upstairs. I check the TV in my room, where I had my game paused all morning. The screen is dark and not in that *you've just died so we're respawning you back to the beginning of the level* dark. I mean, *black* dark.

Like *when your mom's told you to turn off* Dragon Insurgents *seven times already and you keep promising her you're almost done, you just need to clear this last checkpoint so you can save your progress except she runs out of patience, casually strolls into your room, and turns off your TV with zero hesitation* dark.

Yep, *game abruptly over without warning* dark.

Then I'm running back downstairs, flipping light switches, pushing power buttons—but nothing works.

I've barely yanked the front door open when I'm blasted with a sudden burst of fire. Operating on pure instinct, I dive back behind the door for cover, throwing my hands over my face and shielding my eyes against the killer . . .

The killer . . .

The killer . . . glare.

Because . . . sun. It's just . . . sun.

False alarm, but c'mon, to be fair, those sunbeams are *really* intense right now. I just came out of a *pitch-black like the middle of the night, you have no shadow because there is no light* basement.

You know how people sometimes say the sun is *beating* down on us, this is what they meant, this moment. Plus the way it's reflecting off the side of our house, catching our aluminum siding just right, is only making it more . . . is only increasing its feroci . . . you know what, forget it.

Truth serum: It's not just the sun that caught me off guard. It's all of it. Not going to Beach Bash. Mr. Bubbles. The Day Fireworks. Feeling like nobody else is around. The power going out. Getting caught in a dark basement. It's a lot. I'm telling you Bad Luck was looking to take out my knees today.

Anyway, it's broad daylight and as bright as my phone screen in a dark room—which is to say, sunglasses would be cool right about now.

I step back outside, this time fully prepared for the bright light, my eyes already making the necessary adjustments even as I frame my hands around my forehead like a visor and squint at my neighbor's house to the right of ours.

From what I can tell, it's completely dark inside—but that checks out. Mr. and Mrs. Andrews are probably over at Beach Bash stuffing their happy faces with brisket. I heard them talking to my parents about it last week—Mr. Andrews going on and on about how he was ready for some good Ohio barbecue.

The Andrews just moved into the neighborhood a few weeks ago, and apparently wherever they were from—Indiana? Iowa? Idaho? Illinois? I'm pretty sure it's an "I" state—the barbecue was pretty awful. Mom didn't have the heart to tell him that barbecue, let alone good barbecue, isn't exactly Ohio's culinary calling card, especially northeast Ohio. But hey, if you're into ginormous heapings of sauerkraut and jumbo Polish sausages served in a bun *with* coleslaw and fries mashed on top, well, then you've come to the right place!

I look around the cul-de-sac but it's totally empty. Nobody around. And I don't know, somehow the entire street feels so . . . sad. So . . . alone.

Or is that just how I'm feeling right now?

But before I can overthink it too much, I shake the question off and duck back inside the house.

2300

Okay, soooo, what's happening?

We've established it's weird, but yeah, maybe something more specific would be nice.

Off-schedule fireworks in the middle of a sunny day?

A full-fledged, entire-neighborhood power outage (at least from what I can tell via my quick peek outside).

I mean, could it all just be randomness? A complete coincidence? None of it having to do with the other? I mean, yeah, I guess. Except why do I get the feeling there's . . . more?

Why does it feel like there's—

THUUMP! THUUMP! THUUMP!

Umm, what was that?!

THUUMP! THUUMP! THUUMP!

Okay, you heard it, too, yeah?

THUUMP! THUUMP! THUUMP!

Umm, guys, you're still here with me, right?

THUUMP! THUUMP! THUUMP!

Not that I'm scared or anything, I just don't want you to be scared, obviously.

THUUMP! THUUMP! THUUMP!

Wait, wait. Listen. I think . . . I think it's coming from the front of the house. Yeah, it is. I think someone's knocking on the front door.

THUUMP! THUUMP! THUUMP!

Um, yeah—someone's definitely knocking at the door.

I sneak over to the window and try to peek out but they're standing too close to the door, so our porch swing's blocking my view. *Shoot.*

Well, I'm definitely not opening the door if I don't know who it is. Honestly, there's a good chance I wouldn't open it even if I did know. For one thing, we're not supposed to have company over when Mom or WBD aren't home. And secondly, chances are it's not anyone I actually want to see. Everyone I'd want it to be is already at Beach Bash having the time of their lives.

Unexpected Visitor Person raps on the door again—*THUUMP!!*

THUUMP!! THUUMP!!—this time even louder, the sound echoing in my living room as if it were coming from *inside* my house— *THUUMP!!! THUUMP!!! THUUMP!!!*

Whoever it is standing out there on my porch, they seem pretty eager to get someone to come to the door—which in my book is all the more reason *not* to answer it. Oldest trick in *The Book of Old Tricks*—the ole *knock loud as if you have something urgent to say to someone to open the door* trick. Ha, not on my watch, buddy!

But what if it is someone with actual urgent news? What if like Mom sent this person to give me a really important message? What if *gasp*, OMG . . . what if something's happened to Mom (okay, or to WBD, too, I guess)?

Ugh, nope, no, Eddie, not gonna do that! You're not gonna go there! I wag my head trying to shake that thought out of my brain.

Or what if Mom sent a message that she's changed her mind and I *should* come to Beach Bash now after all?

Yeah, right. Does that seem like something my mom would do? It'd be more likely that The Bronster decided to come pick me up to take me out for chocolate chip and pecan cookies because we're best brother-friends now, which is not gonna happen.

THUUMP!!! THUUMP!!! THUUMP!!!

Geez, this person isn't taking silence for an answer. But they'll have to give up eventually, right? All I gotta do is hold my ground and then, I don't know, either they decide to try again later or they scribble a note and leave it on the door. At this point, I don't really care what they do as long as it ends in them leaving . . . like now.

But then the most unexpected thing from the Unexpected Visitor Person happens—

They yell—

"C'mon, I know you're in there! Open the door!"

But they don't just yell, they—

"Open the stupid door, Eddie!"

—yell *my name.*

2400

Okay, so I'm gonna go out on a limb and say there's a decent chance that the stranger on the other side of this door knows me. Either that, or they're freakishly awesome at guessing games.

I'm not sure what this person's dream job is and I'd never encourage someone to ignore their heart—maybe they're dreaming of blasting into outer space and living the zero-gravity life or, I don't know, maybe they wanna do something really cool like become a sandwich artist? That wasn't a joke, sandwich making really is a vital art form. Have you ever tasted a foot-long Italian sub with toasted Parmesan-crusted bread? I rest my case.

Buuuut, if hurtling through black holes or submarine sandwich design don't work out, they could totally be one of those "step right up" folks at the county fair or amusement parks like Cedar Point. You know the people I'm talking about—they're calling after you in one of those semi-truck-looking micro-phones that's pinned to their polo shirt, just as you walk by their booth, offering you a chance to play a really easy and stupendously fun game called *You Stand There and Let Me Stare at You for a Period of Time Just Shy of Super Awkward, at Which Time I Will Wow You and the Gathering Crowd as I Deduce Any of the Following of Your Choosing: Your Age, Your Name, or Your Birthday Month*. The first two, I'll admit, are kinda impressive. The birthday month thing—no offense but that just seems like dumb luck. Plus, if you really wanna—

THUUMP!!! THUUMP!!! THUUMP!!!

Oh, right. The door.

I extend a shaky hand toward the knob.

2500

"If you don't open this stupid door in the next fifteen seconds, I swear . . ."

And okay—I'm sorry. I realize this isn't exactly the best time to jump in here because like, *ohmigod, Eddie, I soooo need to hear the end of that sentence.* Which, fair, and also, me, too. Which is exactly *why* this little time-out is so necessary. Because suddenly this feels like the opportunity to give you a little behind-the-scenes peek into not just Eddie Gordon Holloway: the amazing gamer, the above-average son, and recently failed clothing launderer—nope, this is the perfect moment to reveal Eddie Gordon Holloway: *the man, the poet, the philosopher*—know what I mean?

Huh? What's that? Oh, you *don't* know what I mean *at all*? Well, okay, ummm . . .

Firstly, that's awesome of you to admit that you're lost—seriously, it takes real bravery to speak up and say, *I'm sorry but I just don't get it.* Most of us would rather stay lost than confess we need help, but not you. So, just know, because of *your* emotional vulnerability, in return I am now even more comfy with opening myself up to you, okay? I wanna meet you where *you are*, yeah? I hear you and I see you and I also appreciate you. I'm taking you all in. So anything you wanna say right now, just feel free to express yourself as honestly and as—

Huh? Oh. You . . . you want me to get to the point already?

Okay, well, since we're being honest with each other, it's important that I share with you that what you just said kinda hurt my feelings. I mean, I'm gonna forgive you, but . . . it's just like, I thought we were having a moment and then . . . ouch, you punch me right in the ole figurative kidneys, you know?

But whoops, better get to it, huh?—I'd hate to bore anyone.

All I was gonna say was—when the Unexpected Visitor said: *If you don't open this stupid door in the next fifteen seconds, I swear . . .*

I don't know about you but I instantly had this very visceral reaction.

Like I'm both extremely intrigued and supremely nervous about how that sentence ends—which just goes to show, like, the power of language as a tool of self-expression, you know what I mean?

No, you don't know what I mean?

Okay, well, it's like Mr. Flarts, my fifth-grade English teacher, always said: The best weapon, whether your fight is for love, or survival, or the last piece of 'za in the box—is the element of surprise.

"*. . . I cannot be held responsible for what my hands might do the next time I see you*," the Unexpected Visitor shouts through the door.

My hand takes immediate offense to the threat about *their* hand, so it lets go of the knob, falling back to my side.

Hold up—pause.

Yes, I mostly promise this isn't some weak attempt to delay revealing the Unexpected Visitor's identity. I'd like to take this moment of heightened tension as an opportunity to briefly discuss Very Basic Visiting Etiquette, which I would think is obvious but apparently not so much for whoever's behind door number one. Yes, it's number one because it's the only door.

I gotta say, the fact that this person is now threatening me is definitely decreasing my overall desire to open said door.

In fact, I'm pretty sure the door's gonna remain not-open. Yep, that sounds like the best option.

Although this person is still shouting—which, rude—they are kind enough to decrease their shouting volume, so I'm finally able to truly hear their voice.

And I realize it's a voice I've heard before.

There's a certain familiar *get it together already, Eddie* tone built into it. Even still, I steal another glance out the window to confirm, unlock the door, and swing it open. Except it's barely open two seconds before the screen door is flung open and I'm practically bull-rushed. If not for the floor lamp next to me, 100 percent I would've fallen to the floor.

"Geez, what in the world's going on with you?" I ask.

I watch as the person quickly secures the door behind himself. He stumbles backward, just barely staying upright.

"Are you okay?" I ask. "What's going on?"

But he doesn't answer. Instead, he stays in profile, keeping one side of his face hidden from me.

So I start to repeat my question, except he holds up a finger as if to say, *Give me a sec.* So, I do—which is a little weird in that *okay, now what am I supposed to do, just stand here and look awkward, maybe I should stand with my arms behind my back or is that more awkward, maybe I should lean against the wall opposite, yep, good idea* way—except then I randomly imagine myself falling to the tiled floor and so I just stay where I'm at. The Odd and Uncomfortable Situation Meter's needle swinging to a solid 7 on the *Ugh, I Hate This* index. Standing here listening to his lungs push air out as fast as his body could make it, faster even— while he slumps in our front entranceway, knees bent and sagging just a bit as he starts to catch his breath. Every part of him—from his brown cheeks, reddened and puffy, to his face, neck, and armpits—is all drenched with *I just ran a marathon* level sweat.

"So, you wanna tell me what your deal is, or . . . ?" I ask him as his chest finally stops thumping so hard.

"What's going on with *me*? I'll show you," says my friend Xavier. He turns to face me. And that's when I see it.

2600

It's the all-time worst half-fade, half-fro *hey, bruh, what happened, did your barber keel over dead halfway through, or did you remember after you were already in the chair for twenty minutes that you spent your barbershop money on that burger and fries yesterday, and you try to tell him you'll pay him later when you get more money and he takes the cape off you like cool, I'll finish you later when you get more money, I'm only asking because you look like a broke cartoon character, I'm only asking because you look like you lost an important bet* haircut I, and more than likely this entire universe, have ever seen.

Which is to say, I have a lot of questions and also I have an equal amount of jokes. And since I can't choose which to hit Xavier with first, I choose both.

"Xavier, you ask for that specific cut or did you run out of money and the barber was like, 'Welp you just ran out of a cut, too'?"

"Whatever, bro."

"No, seriously, man, which number is that on the chart so I can ask for the same thing next time I hit up the shop? Wait, lemme guess. It's number one-half." I can barely get the joke out without busting out laughing, but I mean, if you were in my shoes staring at your homeboy and he had *this* haircut, yo, you'd have jokes for dayyyyyyysssssssss.

Plus, me and X always bust each other up. It's how we show love. I'd expect nothing less from him if I were out here looking like I only took half my head to the barbershop and was like, *Huh, what happened to the other half of my head? Oh, it's just at home playing video games. Hey, you still gon charge me for a full cut?*

"Hardy har, very funny. Obviously I was cutting my hair when the power went out, which definitely sucks. Now I gotta go around town looking like a super-broke rapper."

"What, you didn't think to use scissors to at least trim the other side?" I ask.

"What, no, are you kidding me, bro? Shoot, the power went

out and you know how dark my house is even *with* power, so just imagine it without. Bro, it was *pitch-black country road* dark in that bathroom! I dropped the clippers and dashed outta that house like the way you sprinted away from Tasha McKenzie when she asked you to be her boyfriend on Sweetest Day." Now it's Xavier's turn to crack up, and yeah, okay, it's kinda funny. I mean, he's right, I was *up out.* Pumping my arms like I was trying out for the forty-yard dash.

"Whatever, man. I had to take off—you know Tasha runs track. I had to get a head start if I was gonna get away." We both laugh until Xavier's face turns back serious.

"So, scissors, for real? You think?" he asks.

And I see the wheels turning in his brain and I know what he's thinking because he's one of my best friends and we *know* each other—you know what I mean? Like we've been through it all together—summer camp last year, Boy Scouts, the Great Amazing Race (away from Tasha McKenzie)—shoot, you name it, we've done it side by side. True partners, that's what we are.

So, yeah, I see X's face and reading his mind, I know what we gotta do. I slip into the kitchen and reemerge with a pair of scissors from the six-month-old new knife set Mom and WBD got when they got married, because nothing says *eternal love* quite like different-sized knives sticking out of a wooden block, amirite?

But if X had even remotely considered finishing his haircut with scissors, that idea is completely out the window the second he sees them in my hand. He can't shake his lopsided head fast enough, or backpedal quick enough. Clearly, he's gonna pass on my scissor suggestion. I know this because he waves me off and says: "Nah, I'm gonna pass on the scissors, bro. And you're definitely not touching my hair, Shaky Hands Stan."

And I gasp because, not gonna lie, I'm kinda offended. Do I sometimes tremble just a little? Okay, maybe a bit-bit. But Shaky Hands Stan? First of all, it's a terrible insult. Not funny. But also, kind of insensitive.

But, Eddie, weren't you equally insensitive, if not more so, when you kept going on and on and on about Xavier's haircut?

To which I reply once more: Whose side are you on here?

"Wait, how did you even know I was home and not at Beach Bash?"

X studies my face to see if I'm joking. "You really don't know?"

"Know what?" I ask.

He taps his phone and pulls up a saved screen-recording. It's from the Gram. It's The Bronster's latest post. It's a video clip of . . . of . . . no way. Nuh-uh. Please, tell me he didn't.

And because X can also read *my* mind he's all, "Yeah, man, he posted a video of him knocking some pretty gross-looking laundry out of your hands."

I scroll down in horror. "And he captioned it #EddiesGrounded BecauseHe'sAStinkyKid. What the—it has two thousand likes?! How can this be? The Bronster has like three followers."

"That's what I thought when I first saw it, but you gotta admit, he really stepped up his hashtag game on this post," X says.

"Should I report it? Will the Gram people take it down if I report it?"

But X is shaking his head. "You can't, the site is down. Luckily, I managed to grab a copy for . . . my own purposes."

Okay, number one—rude. Now I know my own friend is collecting receipts on me. But X is right. The last thing I wanna do is let The Bronster know his stupid post bothered me even in the slightest. I mean, really, dude? As if I didn't already have enough reasons to hate him, he's like, *Hey, here's a gas station to toss into that forest fire.* Seriously, who would do this to another human, let alone to your own flesh and blood?

"Unfortunately, that's not even the worst part," X says, shaking his head like he wishes he didn't have to be the one to deliver the bad news. "Check who he tagged."

He flips to the next screen grab, and yep, this is most definitely rocketing straight up into the Top 3 on my Worst Nightmares That I Haven't Actually Had But Now That I'm Thinking About It, This Would Be One list:

"He tagged . . ." I swallow hard, the spit burning all the way down my throat. "@AvaBXO."

I recognize that username anywhere: Ava Bustamante.

I shake my head. "Okay, but maybe she didn't see it, right? I mean, she probably gets tagged in lots of stuff, she's one of the most popular girls we know, plus she—"

X points a few rows down from the caption.

AvaBXO: OMG, Eddie, I hope you don't pass out from your own laundry! ☺☺☺

X takes his phone from my stunned (and yes, okay, fine, my also shaky) hands and repockets it with a sympathetic shrug. "Sorry, bro. I tried to text these to you but my phone's acting funny, so."

I pull mine out. It's down to 43 percent with zero service. I've never seen it like this before. Even in the most countriest part of town, I still got a solid three bars. And I know it's a weird time to focus on my phone but I can't help but wonder what else I am missing while it is out of service.

What if the power at the edge of the beach is fine and my mom's trying to get ahold of me right now—except my phone's going straight to voice mail? Even if she left a message, which she loves to do even though I beg her to just text me because who *talks* on phones anymore, gross—I wouldn't be able to listen to it with no signal.

Worse still, what if Ava is texting me and she's wondering why I'm not replying? What if she's getting frustrated with every passing second she didn't hear from me and now she's angrily composing a breakup text like, *lose my number, stinky boy*, even though, you know, we're technically not dating at the moment . . . or at any moment . . . technically. But still.

"Hey." Xavier grips my shoulder. "You all right, man?"

I wag my head. "Yeah, sorry. I'm just . . . I just feel off. Like I've got this strange feeling that I can't explain."

Xavier laughs. "Uh-oh, here we go."

I scoff. "Here we go *what*?"

"You and your strange feelings, that's what. I'm the one walking around like this and you've got strange feelings?"

"No idea what you're talking about."

"No? Lemme jog your memory, my friend. A couple of months ago, the ice cream truck guy? You thought he was casing people's houses so he could break into them and rob them blind? That he was using the old *friendly neighborhood ice cream truck person* as his cover?"

"Umm, are you serious right now?" I throw my hands up in disgust. "He *never* had *Bomb Pops* or *Sundae Cones* or any of those fun *Superhero* Popsicles, like Wolverine or Spider-Man! For like two straight weeks, this dude came around every single day and he only ever had *lemon* Freeze Pops left, talking about, 'Sorry, guys, but I sold out of everything today. But these lemon freezes are great.' Which, first of all, *no one* likes lemon freezes. Lemon ices, okay, I'll give you that. Not my first flavor choice, I'm more of a cherry or strawberry guy myself, but lemon is okay in a pinch. But also, really, bruh? You selling out of all your ice cream every day? Well, then, you must be Ice Cream Truck Business Person of the Year because I've tried to sell things in this neighborhood before. This is not an easy place to move one-dollar chocolate bars, but what, all of a sudden he's handing out five-dollar half-melted ice cream sandwiches like they're going out of style? And hello, my dude, umm, you ever think about carrying *more* ice cream, then? Maybe expanding your inventory, and in turn, increasing your profit margin? I mean, if that's not highly suspicious I don't know what is."

"Are you finished?"

"I don't know. Mostly."

"Go ahead and get it out your system."

"I'm just saying, *lemon* freezes? For real?"

"There were exactly zero break-ins reported."

I shrug. "Clearly, he knew I was onto him, so."

"Eddie, I love you and I'm ridiculously sorry I brought it up, mostly sorry to myself, but you gotta let it go, bro."

I shrug, all out of ideas—and the sad realization that I'm probably gonna miss Beach Bash starts to wash over me, you know, just like those fun lake waves that I'm currently missing out on would've.

2700

"Umm, dude?"

"Yeah, what's up?"

"I get that it's like eight hundred degrees Fahrenheit outside, so I'm more so asking you out of personal concern for *your* comfort level and less so because I'm feeling the slightest bit weirded out about seeing your nipples—"

"Wait, what?" I cut in.

"Not that there's anything particularly wrong with your nipples. That part is definitely more of a *me* problem than it is a *you* issue." His face twists in instant regret. "Not that your nipples are a problem or an issue. I'm trying to say that . . ."

I do a quick scan down at myself.

Xavier clears his throat. "So about this outfit? I know you

didn't get to go to Beach Bash, but why are you still dressed for a volleyball tournament?"

It dawns on me and I refuse to meet his eyes, because here I am, home alone in a bathing suit. And by bathing suit, I mean . . . swim trunks. Only . . . swim trunks.

And by swim trunks, I mean . . . shorter-than-average swim trunks.

As in not anywhere near average length.

Because Ava mentioned she loves my knees, so I just figured I'd be crazy to hide one of my best features, right? If you've got it, flaunt it, right?

Eddie, in what conversational context would Ava Bustamante ever mention a fondness for your bony, ashy knees?

First of all, they're sharp, *not bony*. Two, I'm *not* ashy, but Mom insists on buying the thickest lotion in the history of moisturizers, because she insists we're a dry-skin family—which I'm all *thanks for your concern but speak for yourself, you don't speak for me, I've got my own skin care routine on lock, know what I saying?*—and she's all *I'm so sorry, Eddie. You're right, I really should mind my own business, which is exactly what I'm gonna do, starting right now.* Because Mom knows I don't play.

Eddie, did you actually say any of those things to your mom, or are you exaggerating to impress us?

Umm, I don't exaggerate, let's be clear. And was that an *exact* transcription of me and Mom's lotion conversation? It was definitely the *spirit* of our exchange, not that it's any of your business, so. Point is, the absurdly thick lotion Mom continues to buy is virtually impossible to rub into your body, therefore giving me (and my not-bony-at-all knees) the false appearance of super-ashy skin, when in reality it's just the impenetrable white-gray filmy residue left behind by Mom's awful Skin Blend Lotion—

Which, hello, can you say false advertising?! How are they even allowed to call it *Blend* when it's unblendable? When it only sits on the surface of your skin like oil atop water?

That would be like me saying I'm a professional long-distance swimmer . . . but only in my bathtub.

Plus, I've literally begged Mom to buy Smoketion Potion Love Lotion, a brand scientifically engineered for people with my skin type, it says so on the commercials. *Smoketion Lotion: because you're smoking hot and you should smell like it, too.*

And okay, yes, I possibly heard Ava mention she loves its smell, but so what, it's not a big deal. You really think I'd campaign for my hardworking mom to spend her hard-earned funds on some overpriced, watery lotion just because Ava Bustamante says it smells so good that if Gregory Loganham—one of the weirdest kids in our school, a kid who tucks his T-shirts into his jeans, keeps a pet mouse named Klaus in his front pocket, and never cleans his retainer—started wearing it, she'd probably have to go out with him?

Ha! No way! And actually it offends me that you all would even suggest such a thing.

I start to retreat backward, which I realize is a mistake because I'm still facing X as I leave the room. *How is this my life?* "I'll be right back."

"But with clothes on, right? Right back after you've put on real clothes, is what you mean?"

"Yep, that's the plan . . ." I call over my shoulder, already halfway down the basement stairs.

"But, like, clothes that *I* can also see, yeah?" he shouts from the front door, his voice louder but also muffled, like when you cup your hands around your mouth, except they're also partly covering your mouth, so while you're noticeably louder than when your mouth was hand-cup-less, it's now also harder to understand you—which nearly defeats the purpose of hand-cupping, but hey, what do I know, I'm the guy who thought he had a shirt on.

2700 AND ½

Okay, you're thinking: *Eddie, how could you not realize you're completely shirtless?*

Ugh. I know. It was an honest mistake but this one's all on me. Guess I was so laser-focused on my task—*Laundry! Laundry! Laundry!*—because obviously it's the only thing keeping me from my ultimate goal—*Beach Bash*—that I wasn't exactly operating at peak brain function.

But I'm back now and I'm more self-aware and self-conscious than ever.

2800

In my quickness to retreat, I forgot I was headed back down into the darkness of the basement. But I have to handle this because Xavier is waiting upstairs with half his head shaved.

I turn my phone flashlight back on and cautiously riffle through my heaps of still-unwashed, still-very-dirty clothes. Except the pile's too massive and too precarious—aka it could topple over on me any minute. And I'm pretty sure the last thing I want is to be buried alive in my own dirty garments.

People at my funeral: *You know they found him buried in a mountain of dirty laundry, right? What a way to go. Death by boxer briefs. Sheesh.*

Yep, I can see my tombstone now:

Here lies Eddie, loving son, extremely patient brother, and better-than-average gamer. Eddie left this world under the weight of his own soiled laundry, his last few breaths were of his own sweat-tinged, tear-inducing stink. Eddie is survived by his favorite (dirty) jeans, his vintage Mighty Moat (best band ever) (also dirty) T-shirts, and his family. Eddie's last and dying wish was that we emphasize he'd still be with us today if his mom hadn't grounded him from Beach Bash—not that he wants her to feel guilty. Okay, maybe a little guilty. Also, sup, Ava, you looking cute.

I give a few items the good ole sniff test, but truth is, you can smell them from Jupiter (my bad, Jupiterians!).

Point is this—I was embarrassed to admit this earlier, but during that clothes-valanche scene with Mom this morning? Yeah, I nearly blew chunks, the smell was so bad. Which is weird, right, because it's not as if they weren't in my closet the entire time. You'd think such a putrid smell would've been nauseating me weeks ago when the only barrier between it and me was a cheap, faux (fancy for fake!) wood closet door.

It sucks but at this point I've gotten so used to it I've practically developed an immunity against it. Kinda like how I deal with The Bronster. Obviously, the best-case scenario would be The Bronster didn't exist, but since that's not in the cards, the next best thing is: *ignore ignore ignore.*

And yeah, not exactly a sophisticated plan, but it's gotten me this far. I've survived this long. Except now it was coming to bite me in the bottom. And no, not just nibble nibble release. No, we're talking a Sharkzilla, *oops, looks I swallowed you whole, sorry, that's my bad* bite.

Because it turns out that my amazing, perfectly crafted, once-in-a-lifetime plan has now backfired on me twice. First, Mom banning me from Beach Bash because of the laundry. And now every single article of clothing I own is either filthy, wet, or locked in a washing machine with no power.

I step back out of the basement in nothing but my swim trunks, waiting for X to notice.

"So that's a 'no' on more clothes, then?"

"Bro, for real? You really gonna talk about me right now? Dude, you look like a confused porcupine—*well, gee, guys, do I push out all my quills or maybe just half?*" I say in my best porcupine-sounding voice.

"Your porcupine voice sucks. Like really bad."

I fold my arms across my chest. "Whatever. Can't you see I'm in the middle of a laundry crisis here?"

The eyebrow on the fro-half of X's head slides upward—a

single-eyebrow raise like our favorite pro wrestler does. It's a move that X knows makes me wildly jealous because when it comes to movement, my eyebrows are apparently a package deal only. *Your eyebrows are like couples' ice-skating. They only move together or not at all*, X once said after a particularly painful session whereby I kept attempting to force one brow up and asking him *Did I do it?* for like two hours. It's a wonder he didn't run out my house screaming, but nope, he just kept answering, *Not quite, man, sorry.* I guess that's why we're friends, we know how to handle each other.

"No clean clothes," I confess with a frown.

"None? Nothing? Not one sock?"

"You got it."

"Well, what about borrowing something from your brother?"

"Um, did you forget what happened the last time I borrowed just a pair of old socks?"

X nods. "Oh, shoot, he filled your sheets with honey and then made back up your bed . . ."

I sniff the air. "That was two months ago and fifty percent of everything *still* smells like honey. That was socks. If he comes back and sees me in his actual clothes, it'll be a beehive under my blankets next time."

"Fair," X says. "And what about your stepdad's closet? Is that empty, too?"

"No way I'm going there. He dresses like a total nerd. He looks like he's the host of a show entirely dedicated to grandfather clocks. It's a hard pass."

"Okay, well, what about your mo—"

I cut him off. "Don't do it. Don't even ask me about my mom. I'd rather stay in this and my flip-flops."

"What about your sneakers?" Xavier suggests.

"Which makes sense, except they're a bit stinky and I don't have any clean socks, so if I wear them sock-less my feet are gonna stink, too."

Xavier grins at me in that way he does when a joke is coming. "News flash, my friend, you're too late."

We walk outside and I am feeling super-duper thankful that it's hot as a clenched hairy armpit today. Seriously, imagine if it were one of those out-of-nowhere summer days where it's suddenly forty degrees and cloud city? No way I could venture outside without freezing my thin, swim-trunked butt off!

Moral of the story: Things could be infinitely worse, which in my experience is an attitude/outlook that's great to have. No matter how bad things get, no matter how awful things turn, there are likely a hundred other situations far more horrendous than yours. In fact, at that very moment you're feeling sorry for yourself, someone else is actually going through far more horrendous things, and so, in the immortal words of the most adventurous, most daring human I know, my Nana Charlie, *Better buck up, buckaroo.*

Still, I wish I had a clean T-shirt. *Sigh.* But okay, Nana, you win (as always). Let's go figure this thing out.

2900

We decide to take our bikes and scout the neighborhood. The way we see it, if we're both stuck at home without power, there's probably others, yeah? Plus, maybe we'd find someone with a working phone.

Annnnddd I'd be willing to bet that if I called my parents and explained the situation—that as much as I really, really wanted to finish my laundry—this whole deal was beyond my control now. The mighty Electricity gods have spoken and they have declared *there will be no more juice for you*—and since there's no way to know *how* long this power outage is gonna last (I've heard of these things lasting for days! Weeks!), I mean, they'd have to cave and let me go to Beach Bash, amirite?

When it came down to it even the most unreasonable person would make the right decision here and fold, yeah?

Ahhh, I can see it now, me kicked back in my beach chair, minding my own biz, when Ava Bustamante appears out of nowhere and she's like, *Oh wow, those swim trunks are niiice, Eddie,* but like I know she really means my knees. And I just take a long sip of my Triple Berry Tongue Slap Your Brain Stupid Silly Super Slushie and shrug like she's the seventeenth person to compliment my trunks and then super casually I say something cool like, *Cool, thanks.* Flash her a smile, maybe ask her to join me at the volleyball court. Okay, okay, but a guy can dream, right? Besides, anything's possible. Ava just needs to spend time with me and realize that maybe I'm not the coolest, or smoothest, or cutest, or most athletic, or smartest, or tallest, or fastest, or most coordinated, or—okay, you get the picture—but what I lack for in those categories, I more than make up for with my . . . with my . . .

Point is, I just gotta get there and whatever happens happens. Oh yeah, I can practically feel that cool lake breeze blowing across my face.

And then I see Xavier wildly waving his hands, trying to get my attention. And then I realize that relaxing sea breeze that felt so very real—yeah, that's just him blowing on my face. "Earth to Eddie, Earth to Eddie, are you there?"

"Dude, you got spit in my eye," I say, taking a step back as I dramatically wipe wet air molecules from my face. "What's the plan?"

"Maybe we split up," Xavier suggests. "You take north of Ellison Avenue and I'll head south? And we'll meet back here in thirty minutes?"

I nod my agreement and Xavier taps his MeWatch screen, checks the time. I set my own MeWatch timer. "See you in thirty," I say, already pedaling in the opposite direction.

"Hey, that's south," Xavier yells behind me. "You're going north!"

And I throw my hand up in acknowledgment and hit a U-turn.

"I knew that," I tell him as we zoom past each other.

"Obviously," he agrees.

3000

Most kids in our hood live either on the street in front of our Ellison Ave cul-de-sac or on the street behind it—so it makes sense to start our split-up and head in both directions. And, duh, of course, Xavier opted to take the southern route. It's the logical move because (1) that's his part of our hood, his family lives in that direction and (2) and maybe most importantly—no one knows those streets like X.

But even more importantly, Xavier knows *every* single person in *every* single house. Honestly, he could've gone north, too, because he probably knows *my* neighbors better than I do.

I turn down Lois Lane, a street name that always makes me grin—shout-out to Superman! I speed up past the first two houses, both well known for their watchdogs—although, both are eerily super quiet. Maybe the dogs went to Beach Bash, too?

Halfway down the block, I hit 343 (the Lawrence twins' house) with a quick pedal-by of their side yard. The Lawrence twins always stash their bikes behind a tall row of flowery shrubs. Yesterday, they asked me if I was taking my bike to Beach Bash because they'd convinced their mom to let them ride around the boardwalk—so if the bikes aren't there, then neither is Torry or Terry.

That's okay, though, because I didn't really come this way to find the twins. They just happen to live next door to . . . you guessed it . . . Ava Bustamante.

It's a long shot that she's home, but I push the doorbell anyway. How many times have I thought about this moment? Dreamed of walking up the stairs and standing on this porch, waiting for someone—hopefully her—to open the door?

I don't know what it is, but it's always been hard for me to meet new people. It's not because I don't want to make new friends. I love people, but I guess I'm just nervous they won't love me back? I know what you're thinking, *Umm, what's up, because this definitely doesn't sound like the same confident, secure Eddie we've come to know and love?*

But I promise you, it's still me. I guess the thing is it just takes me a little longer to feel comfortable enough with someone new to show them the real Eddie. Okay, okay, I'm equally uncomfortable with opening up with people who aren't new, too. Like Ava Bustamante—I've known her since her family moved to Carterville in second grade and she slid into the only seat left in our class— yep, right next to mine. Even then, when she sat down on her first day, looked across the aisle at me, and smiled—I struggled to even look her in the eye. Okay, to be real, I *didn't* look her in the eye. I kept my eyes as far away from hers as I could, pretending to admire the dirty orange tile floor until she finally looked away.

So I've known Ava for nearly half my life but as far as crushing on her—I'll tell you it's a new thing, that it's only been since the end of this past school year. But the actual truth? It started that day in second grade.

I hear footsteps and my heart speeds up—a few drops of sweat glide down my cheek. Between the sun and my own internal heat ramping up, another few minutes of this and I'll be officially saturated.

The footsteps grow louder and now I'm shaking—buzzing with anticipation. What should I say? What if she's not only *not* surprised to see me, she's unhappy, too?

Dang, maybe I should leave? Maybe this was a mistake?

But then I realize no one's coming to the door.

Those footsteps? Yeah, false alarm—those were coming from behind me.

Could it be Ava, coming back to her house just to see me standing at her front door?

Nah.

It's my best friend, Sonia, walking down the street with dead eyes, holding an unplugged video game controller, and she's chanting the same thing over and over again:

"Here comes the super sludge nightmare machine, hope you're hungry. Here comes the super sludge nightmare machine, hope you're hungry . . ."

3100

"Sonia, are you okay?" I say, shaking her a little.

Her eyes have a faraway, glassy look to them—and no, not *just* because she wears glasses. Seriously, she could be the cover model for a zombie magazine right about now.

"Sonia, the power went out. Is that what happened at your place, too?"

Something flickers in her eyes. "Pow," she mumbles.

"Huh?" I ask. "I don't understand, Sonia."

"Were," she mutters.

"Sonia, sheesh, I'm gonna need you to snap out of it like right now because this whole thing where you mumble random things is not it."

But Sonia says both words again, this time closer together,

and now it's clear what she means. "Power," I repeat. She's saying *power*. "Sonia, you lost power, too?"

Sonia just barely nods. Well, it's either a nod or her head's getting too heavy for her neck. "Must be restored, the power," Sonia says, far more crisply this time.

"Yes, tell me about it. Any ideas how we do that?" I ask her.

Except she's back to full-on zombie mode. Back to "Here comes the super sludge . . ."

See, Sonia's one of those *everybody loves her* type people. But that's not hard to understand, seeing how Sonia is probably the realest person I've ever met. Seriously, she's never fake. You always know where you stand with her. And she treats everyone the same—no matter how rich or not rich you are, no matter if you live in the worst house or the best, if you're this color or that, or funny or super serious. She also has zero tolerance for stupidity. We've been best friends since we were wobbling for our very first steps. No one knows us the way we know each other. But even with our history, Sonia doesn't hesitate in calling me out. Sonia's tough but also fair. Like I said, she's always real.

"We gotta get you back to reality," I said.

I point to the two bars jutting from the rear wheel. Sonia and I do this all the time. It's the easiest way for two people to ride a bike.

"Hop on, my zombie power-restoring friend, hop on. We've got places to go and people to . . . Okay, we don't have people to see. It doesn't matter. I screwed it up, but what else is new, right? C'mon, let's get out of here, yeah?"

By the time she and I make it back to my house, Xavier's already there, his bike lying on its side in the middle of my driveway. I hop off my bike and let it fall into the grass.

That's when I see Xavier's found a couple new friends of his own. Trey Davis, also known as the best athlete in all of Carterville of *any* grade. Along with his younger sister, whose name I always struggle to remember. Wait, let me think, it's something like Shoney, or Shawna, or . . .

"Sage," a voice says, knocking me from my thoughts. It's Trey's sister, grinning at me. "My name's Sage but you were close," she assures me.

I nod. Sage, yes, why can't you ever remember that, Eddie? It's only four letters, bro. And why would you play GUESS WHAT HER NAME IS right in front of her, ummm, rude—

Except wait . . . hold up . . .

Had I actually spoken any of that out loud?

No, I'm fairly certain it had all been in my head, but then that doesn't make much sense because how would Sage know what I'd been thinking?

I look back over at her and she's got her eyes locked in on me. Most of her face is filled up by her large smile, her braids constantly falling across her face and both of her hands working overtime to keep them pushed back.

I study her a beat before I ask, "So, how'd you do that?"

She wags her head. "I don't understand. How did I do what exactly?"

I give her a look like, *Really, stop playing.* But she says nothing more, her face doing all the talking like, *Ask if you wanna ask, dude.* "You knew exactly what I was thinking? How?"

Xavier laughs. "Ohmigod, bro, how is it she knew what you were thinking? That you didn't know her name? Anyone looking at you could see that."

And everyone joins in the laughter, me included. "Okay, fair. But wait, how did you know I was guessing the name wrong, too?"

The laughter stops. "I mean, it's all over your face."

I can't help but nod, the same way I can't help but be impressed by this kid. I mean, she can't be any older than eight, maybe . . .

"Nine," Sage says. "I'll be ten in three months."

I shake my head in disbelief—not at her age but at this ridiculous talent. "Okay, you've gotta teach me your ways."

She tosses me the mature, confident wink of a human three times her height and five times her age. "I got you. No problem."

"So it looks like this is it. In all of Carterville, we five are the lone holdovers from Beach Bash," Xavier says with a smile.

"Not a bad fivesome if I do say so myself," I say, pacing back and forth with my arms behind my back, the same way I've always dealt with new challenges or circumstances.

"How come you two didn't go to Beach Bash?" I ask Sage and Trey.

"You want me to tell it, or . . . ?" Sage waits for her brother to start.

And I'm not sure, it could just be the angle I'm standing at and the fact that Trey is like eight feet taller than me, but it looks like his bottom lip is trembling. But that doesn't make sense. That's what you do when you're nervous or afraid or . . . cold?

But we can rule out cold because, hello, it's triple digits hot out here!

But why would Trey be nervous, let alone afraid?

I think back to the last time I saw Trey—

—the final week of school. It was the championship game after he led our middle school basketball team to an un-defeated regular season *and* postseason. He was going off, as always, scoring what felt like every big basket, dishing out every huge assist. The kid was on fire, but what else was new? He's easily the best athlete our school has ever seen and it's not even close.

"I . . . I didn't . . ." Trey stammers. Which is also weird because Trey doesn't stammer. He's the most confident kid I've ever known.

Whatever's going on with him, it's clearly connected to all this other weird stuff. Maybe something crazy happened to him when their power went out, too.

Trey is still trying to get out the words when his little sister swoops in and explains everything for the both of them. "I mean, the truth is, Trey should be there. He's only stuck home because I didn't wanna go and Mom and Dad made him stay with me. Apparently even though I'm old enough to be at home by myself during the week when Mom and Dad are still at work and Trey hasn't gotten back from school yet, but not today. I don't know what the difference is."

"I'll tell you what the difference is," Trey says with a sigh. "During the week you're home alone for like twenty minutes. Not twelve hours."

Sage nods her head like *good point*. "Okay, well, it's not like you're gonna have to stay with me the entire day. Mom said they'd come back later this afternoon and then you can go be with your friends."

Trey shrugs. "We'll see. No big deal."

"What's up with her?" Sage nods at Sonia, who is still hitting buttons on her control pad.

"She's been playing *Monster Hunters II* for the last four weeks. I think she was close to beating it when the power went out. She's having trouble separating from the game."

"Well, it's no weirder than his haircut, I guess," Sage says, pointing at the left side of Xavier's head.

"Sonia, do you hear us? Nod if you can hear us," Xavier says into Sonia's ear.

But nothing doing. She's still stuck on that same line: "Here comes the super sludge nightmare machine, hope you're hungry. Here comes the super sludge nightmare machine, hope you're hungry . . ."

X and I exchange looks like, *What should we do?*

And we both answer with simultaneous shrugs, which is pretty much our go-to move.

And then it hits me and I say four magical letters: "WWSD."

X one-eyebrows me, the show-off. "What does that mean?"

I grin as I make one all-in attempt to one-eyebrow-raise him back but he just shakes his head and frowns. "Bro, I hate that you're trying so hard right now."

So, I quit the terrible facial expression and refocus on my letters. "What would Sonia do?"

X scrunches his face in confusion. "Okay, that's a good question but what is WWSD?"

And I've never actually done this before—outside of using the emoji for it—but yeah, I break him off a super-emphatic face-palm. "WWSD *is* what would Sonia do."

I see the light come back on in his eyes. "Ohhhh. Makes sense. After all, she's clearly the smart one in our group."

Not gonna lie, I wanna argue this point but he's right; she is the smart one.

X squints at me like he's waiting for me to finish. "So, what would she do?"

And even though I instantly hate myself for doing it, I wink at him. "Ha, more like what *wouldn't* Sonia do?"

For whatever reason, in situations where things are new or intense or both, pacing the room has always helped. It has a way of slowing my brain down just enough to process whatever needs processing while managing the anxiety. "But here's the real question, here we are, the five of us alone and unsupervised, with literally our entire neighborhood at our disposal—so then what should we do with our new freedom, my friends?"

Everyone takes a second to think before even attempting a reply—

Which I take as a good thing—a sign that everyone's taking this opportunity seriously.

But then a few moments pass with nothing but silence. I scan everyone's face. I grin and my mouth starts to open in response but then I catch myself and motion at Sage to take the floor. "Sage, you wanna take it from here?"

She shakes her head like maybe she's a little embarrassed or just confused. "Umm, what am I even supposed to do?" she says.

"You wanna tell everyone what I'm thinking or is it all me this time?"

Sage grins hard. "You got this one. I'll take the next."

3200

Sonia is my BFF and so that means I have to hook her up. That's what I do. You know this. My friend is stuck in a game that she was close to beating but just didn't get a chance to finish up the final level.

We gotta get her out, and there's only one way to do it.

Plus, Sonia's smart. She'll probably know what to do about this no-power situation.

"Wait, hold on, you want *us* to do *what*?" Xavier asks, his shoulders hunched in that *I don't get it because I actually don't wanna get it* way that absolutely drives me crazy—even though, okay, yes, I'm occasionally guilty of it, too—geez, you guys, I admit it, okay. But the major diff is: I do *not* use the shoulder hunch all willy-nilly. I'm not just tossing shoulder hunches out left and right like they're going out of style. Nope. I respect that gesture and therefore I only resort to it when it is absolutely necessary.

Like when Mom tells me to do something I don't feel like doing.

Like sheesh, be responsible, you know what I'm saying?!

"We're gonna play *Monster Hunters II* . . . except IRL," I explain *for the fourth time.* "Sonia put her heart into that game all summer and what, you think we're just gonna let it get flushed down the toilet because of some stupid power outage? No stinkin' way!"

"Wait, are you saying we're gonna . . ."

"Yep." I nod, my smile widening by the second. "Bring the game to life."

"Just making sure I heard you over how loud your bathing suit is," Xavier says.

"Yeah, I get it, you probably still have hair in your one ear," I come right back at him.

"Power, restored it must be," Sonia mutters.

"Exactly, Sonia. It's time we take back our power. And if we're gonna do this thing, we're gonna do this right," I tell everyone.

And all their faces twist into confusion like, *Uh-oh, what's*

Eddie talking about, and why do we get the feeling that whatever it is, it's 100 percent gonna be wild and crazy? Everyone except Sonia, because she's still staring off into Monster Land like this driveway is the Vampire Volcano. And then I'm turning on my flip-flop heels and racing toward my house like I'm on fire, all of them flinging questions at my back, like:

Sage: *Why are you running?*

Xavier: *Do you have to poop?*

Trey: *Hm.*

Sonia: *Use your Monster Mash before you die and lose it!!*

But I don't stop to answer because I'm a kid on a mission and I will not be stopped. And because I don't know what Sonia is saying!

But no matter how deep she is into this, even if I have to drag her kicking and screaming out of her hallucination, I will do whatever it takes.

Here I am—flying through our living room, sliding across our kitchen floor, and diving through the heavy basement door. I'm halfway down the stairs when I throw on the brakes and grab at my face because, ugh, here I am, back in the dark basement again.

I've probably been down here more in one day than in the last year combined.

I can't *see* anything.

Not one ounce of light. I turn my phone light on again— 22 percent now.

With every step I take, descending farther into the basement, the more *your entire wardrobe of dirty laundry is down here* smell hits me in the nostrils.

It's very . . . weird.

But then, over in the far dark corner, I spot the whole reason for even being down here in the first place—

Three big cardboard boxes stacked on top of each other.

I walk over and examine the top box. I smile. *Bingo.*

3300

The four of them huddle around me (or the three of them and Sonia, who is sort of just aimless) as I carefully set the cardboard box in the grass in between two of the pink penguins.

I drag the sharp tip of my house key down the middle of the box, slicing through the layers of thick packing tape. I pop open each flap and everyone scoots in closer.

"What is it?" Sage asks.

I pull the top item from the box and hold it up for all to see—X takes it from my hands and holds it in front of his face.

"It's a mask," he says.

Sage nods excitedly. "It's a zombie! Lemme see." She slips the mask over her face and groans. "How do I look?"

"Terrifying," I assure her.

"What else is new?" Trey mumbles under his breath.

Sage lowers the mask and stares Trey down. "I heard that. *Not* cute."

Xavier stoops beside me, reaching into the box and pulling out another mask—this time a mummy. I dig into the box and hold up the rest of Sage's zombie costume and her eyes light up, her small hands clapping in genuine happiness.

"There's something for everyone," I say, stepping away from the box to make room for the others. "Dig in."

I reach in and grab the only thing I need. A set of plastic fangs. Now I'm a vampire in a bathing suit.

3400

Level 1 starts in my garage.

Which I admit is risky.

You know, considering WBD's most prized possession is also in the garage.

"You think your stepdad will ever let you drive it?" Mummy X asks, lifting up the car cover to take a peek. I smack his hand.

"Ow!" he shouts. "That hurt!"

"I'm sorry, but unless you're trying to get me grounded until I'm one hundred and twenty-two, I'm gonna have to remind you that absolutely, under no circumstances is anyone to touch this car?"

"Dude, I just wanted to *look*."

"No looking, either, my friend. Don't even breathe on it."

Mummy X shrugs. "What's the point of having a sweet ride if you're just gonna keep it locked up in your garage? Why didn't he drive it to Beach Bash?"

I laugh. "Mom hates riding in it because he's so busy making sure no one is messing with anything, he doesn't pay attention to the road."

"It's a Thunderbird, right?"

I nod. "Betsy the Thunderbird."

Mummy X whistles. "What I wouldn't do to take this bad boy for a spin . . ."

"X! Focus, before you get drool all over it and we both die." I nudge him back in Sonia's direction. "Besides, we've got a game to play. Or should I say, *Sonia's* got a game to play."

"Power," Sonia drones.

"Remember," I say, looking my friend in her zombie eyes. "You must complete the task assigned for each level and collect a gold coin"—I hold up a plastic gold coin the size of my fist—"before you can move on to the next."

"Okay, okay, are you ready to get this game started?" Mummy X asks.

"I must," Sonia says. "The power."

I squeeze her shoulder and look her in her eyes. "Don't forget, just like in the real game, you only get three lives."

Sonia nods, kind of.

"Are you sure this is gonna work? That she's up for this?" X says as we race to our positions.

"Good luck," I call over my shoulder to Sonia before turning back to X. "I really hope so."

And his face flashes concern but I kick it into high gear and dash into my spot.

And, okay, yes, it takes Sonia a while to get going, I admit. She sorta just stumbles out of my garage, but at least she heads in the right direction.

She's halfway down the driveway when Sage the Zombie starts sprinting toward her full speed, waving a light-up plastic sword from last Halloween when I went as a space cadet. Sage the Zombie lets rip her best battle cry: "HFLKJHKLDGJKLJFSKLJFKLSJKLJFSK!"

For a second, I think about looking away—because it becomes abundantly obvious what's about to happen. Sonia, my friend since forever, is not only gonna stay in her own zombie mode, she's about to get zonked in the face with a fake lightsaber at the hands of a super-talkative fourth grader. I mean, you can see it all lining up, in slow motion—

I try to tell Sage to slow down but it's too late, the sword's already extended like Sage means to play Home Run Derby with Sonia's dome . . .

. . . and it's too late, the sword is already connecting, except it misses Sonia's face, walloping the back of her head instead with a loud *WHOOOOMP!*

But then something happens.

I don't know if it's the head shot she just caught like a champ, or the hundred-degree weather, or the fact that a munchkin zombie is attacking her and Sonia's pride just goes into autopilot. All I know is: Something flickers in Sonia's eyes and suddenly she's alive.

Sage is already winding up for another hard blow, but this time Sonia sidesteps the saber and extends her palm into Sage's chest as if to stun her.

"You sleepy, friend? After all, *zzzzz* is for *zombie*, right?" Sonia says. And Sage stumbles backward to the ground, her hand shooting up with something sparkling in it as she lies defeated in the grass. It's the first coin and Sonia smiles. "Looks like you won't be needing this," she says, taking the coin from Sage's hand and pocketing it. She bends over and takes Sage's saber. "Or this. Sweet dreams, Zombie Girl."

And then Sonia's racing off.

She's sprinting through the yard when suddenly Trey leaps out from behind a big oak tree. It's strangely an awkward landing for someone with Trey's athleticism, but whatever, we're playing a video game in our yards. I think he gets a pass.

"Not so fast, Monster Hunter," Trey says, scowling. He tosses his head back and lets loose the most bloodcurdling howl I've ever heard. "AWWWOOOOOOOOOOO!"

Sonia laughs. "Cute—are you supposed to be a stray dog or something?"

Trey shakes his head as he pulls out his two Death Discuses, one in each hand (which are really just my long-distance Frisbees, but hey, it works). "We'll see how cute you think I am after I eat your bones for lunch, Hunter."

"My bones, huh?" Sonia says with a smirk. "Come and get 'em, Wolfie."

But Trey's already unleashed a blue Frisbee from his right hand. It zips through the sky, glancing Sonia's ear and forcing her to turn her head. By the time she regains her balance, Trey's whipping the other discus, this one catching her in the leg, and she goes down hard.

"Oh darn," Trey says, walking toward his fallen victim. "Lunch is here and I forgot my knife and fork." He picks up the blue Frisbee from the grass. "No mind, I'll just use—"

"Monster Hunter Homie!" Sonia screams on her back.

And then in an explosion of speed and light, Zoras the Monster Hunter Homie appears, ramming directly into Trey's gut, catching him completely by surprise.

"Wait, who's Monster Hunter Homie?" Trey asks, stunned.

"Every level you get one special super friend appearance," Sonia explains. "They're called your Monster Hunter Homie."

And this Monster Homie is none other than . . . Xavier. He takes a bow. "Zoras the Homie, at your service, Monster Hunter. I think you've got it from here," he says, grinning as he pulls Sonia up from the ground. She takes the gold coin from Trey's outstretched hand and steps over his discuses.

"Until next time, Homie," she says, fist-bumping Zoras as she turns to survey the land ahead. I reinsert my vampire teeth and when I look up she's already zooming toward me.

I wanna tell you that I stand up to Sonia the mighty Monster Hunter, that she's no match for my Vampire Vexes—tennis balls that I hurl at her from the two buckets on either side of me as I hide in the bushes.

I only narrowly miss her and she laughs. "Nice try, Vamps. Or should I say *Gramps*."

"Oh, I'm only getting started," I assure her. I reach down for more ammo but when I pop back up she's vanished.

"Hey, where'd you go? Got you on the run, huh, Monster Hunter? Running scared as I knew you wou—"

Except I don't get the full sentence out of my lips when something latches onto my ankles, and I crash to the ground.

How did this happen, you ask?

My best friend, Sonia, just happened is the short answer.

The longer one? Oh, nothing special, she just decided to pull off the kick-butt move of the century—that's all.

I can't even get back to my feet before she's pelting me with a dizzying array of kicks and punches (clearly holding back because, duh, she doesn't actually want to hurt me) and I play along, loudly grunting *UGH* with each blow.

Until she reaches into the buckets and throws two perfect

balls right for my head, both ricocheting off my face, the first one catching me in the nose, and the second one landing right in the kisser, knocking free my vampire teeth and sending them sailing through the sky.

She stands over me, smiling triumphantly, the sun gleaming off her shoulders behind her. She extends her hand to me and for a second I think she's back to being my friend again, that she's helping me up to my feet, but naturally, I couldn't be more wrong.

"Ahem," she says, clearing her throat and knocking away my empty hand. "Aren't you forgetting something?"

"Yeah, yeah, yeah, fine, you win, whatever," I say, holding out the final gold coin, which she snatches from my hand.

And maybe it's just sweat but I swear I see a tear or two in her eyes. "I did it," she says. "I've restored the power."

I nod from the ground. "You did it, Monster Hunter Sonia. You are the greatest Hunter on Planet Xagostia."

"Thank you. You're not wrong," Sonia says, now helping me up for real this time. "Not that anyone's surprised by my superior fighting skills."

I roll my eyes. "Oh, boy," I say, my voice dripping in sarcasm.

But in reality, I'm ecstatic because, just like that, Sonia, my wise and wisecracking friend, is back!

I smile at her. She smiles at me, and the other three as they walk up the driveway toward us.

Sonia shakes her head in disbelief, then stares down at her three gold coins. "I can't believe you did all this for me."

"Eh, you'd do the same for us." I shrug. "It's no big deal."

"Well, it's a big deal to me, so."

"Awww, you two are so cute," Sage sings, clasping her hands together.

But Xavier interrupts, as usual. "Guys, as touching as this little moment is . . . and believe me, my heart's seven degrees of melty right now," he says, clutching his chest super dramatically, ". . . but, uh, yeah, it's *way* too hot to have on these bandages."

"What's up with his hair?" Sonia asks me.

"Umm, hello, why are you asking Eddie like I'm not standing right here next to you?" X whines. Sonia throws her arms around X's shoulders and he pretends to try to pull away but he lets her squeeze him.

"Awww, X, you know I love you," Sonia says.

We're all feeling the love now except we'd nearly forgotten the best part of the entire game.

"But wait, there's more," I exclaim and Sonia shoots me a quizzical look like, *Ummm, what are you talking about? Did I hit you too hard on the head with those tennis balls?*

"Guys," I say as Sage, Trey, and X—and me—form a circle around our victorious hunter. "One and a two and a one, two, three . . ."

And all together, in not-so-perfect harmony, the four of us bellow out the best video game theme music ever written.

"Monster Hunter, she doesn't mess around. Monster Hunter never stays down. If you see the Monster Hunter, and you're a monster, might we suggest you leaavvveee toowwwnnnnn . . ."

And we all crack up laughing and maybe for just a minute I manage to forget about Beach Bash while there are whole video games happening in the front yard.

3500

If you're like me, video games definitely level up your appetite.

Honestly, I almost never pick up a controller without first securing as many awesome snacks as I can hold in:

- **My arms.** My go-to snack-carrying system, arms get the job done. And they're great for carrying cookies, bowls of kettle corn, or a bag of my favorite sour gummies.

- **My pockets.** Seems obvious, right? But in the heat of slyly snagging snacks—say that three times fast—people panic and forget that pockets are built-in stash spots for fruit snacks, juice boxes, or a bag of my favorite sour gummies.

- **My teeth.** Yep, you heard me—my teeth. Pro tip: If you're not using your teeth as an extra mode of snack transportation, you're only hurting yourself. Seriously, your chompers are perfect for clenching small chip bags or, you know, a bag of sour gummies, ha!

And you're like, *Ummm, Eddie, you could also not be lazy and make multiple trips.*

Except this isn't about laziness, my friends (although tbh, energy conservation should always be our goal). No, this is about good ole-fashioned common sense, which, as Nana Charlie loves to say, *is not very common at all*, ha.

Here's the scenario: You've already completed a couple of round-trip deliveries, successfully relocating your favorite goodies from the stash spot to your room—a job well done, right? But you're not satisfied, worse still, you're overconfident, so now you press your luck and make a third or fourth run.

You take more chances, push the limit, really start feeling yourself, and then suddenly, BOOM, you've attracting unwanted parental-unit attention.

Hey, hey, wait a minute, where do you think you're going with all that junk food?

And as you're forced to hand over the goods, you realize all this could've been avoided if you'd only consolidated and used all your available resources—arms, pockets, and, yep, your teeth! But you only have yourself to blame. You flew too close to the sun, my friend. You practically begged them to hassle you. So, remember: the less back-and-forth, the better.

Especially if you have my mom—or as she's known around our neighborhood: The Snack Time Terminator.

Good luck sneaking anything past Mom, ha. Forget the back of her head, she's got eyes on both sides, too. So, smuggling junk food? Basically impossible. It's easier to grab an FBI laptop filled with top secret spy files than chips or cookies from our pantry.

Most days, she's all, *Here, son, have some delicious celery stalks.*

And you're like, *Eddie, celery's a classic snack food staple. We've been down with celery sticks since preschool, my man.*

Except Mom wants me to eat celery . . . without peanut butter or veggie dip! O THE CRUELTY! O THE INJUSTICE!

MOM: *Eddie, why even eat healthy foods, if you're gonna pair it with processed sugars and salts?*

Which is *my* question exactly, Mom—why even eat healthy foods?

But also, if you're not supposed to scoop a glob of pb or dip with your celery stick, then how come they've got that empty "please fill me with stuff" groove down the middle?

Look, you all count on me for the truth, no matter how ugly, so here it is:

Yes, in theory it's good to eat foods that make you, in Nana Charlie's words, *big and strong with magazine-model skin.* But where healthy food goes super wrong is the taste.

Healthy food usually sucks. The textures are weird, the smell's awful, and their presentation isn't doing them any favors. Face it: You set cauliflower side by side with a triple chocolate chunk cookie and it's not even fair.

Even healthy food names are terrible!

Brussels sprouts: First of all, where can I find this Brussels person, because I've definitely got beef with them. And two, doesn't *Brussels sprouts* sound like a verb? As in, they're gonna *keep on sprouting* even after you've eaten them? And you're like, *Eddie, you lost me when you interjected the grammar lesson.* I'm just saying, how are you gonna feel when weeks later you're laughing with your friends and then, *WHOOSH*, green leaves are shooting outta your mouth?!

Asparagus: C'mon, this joke writes itself.

Broccolini: 100 percent a corny cartoon bad guy. I, Broccolini, am the Vilest Vegetable Villain in all of Gardenia, and also one of your parents' best friends, and you kids aren't going anywhere until you've eaten *every last veggie on your plate, muhahahaha (or whatever over-the-top evil maniacal laughter sounds like).*

In summation: Healthy food's gross. Sugary, salty, processed, *is this even real food* food? Stupid delicious.

And as usual, Sonia and I are on the same page.

"You thinking what I'm thinking?" I ask her.

Her eyes brighten with excitement. "Snack raid?"

I smile. "Have I told you lately how much I love your brain?"

And everyone quickly, happily agrees with our plan and just like that, Operation Treat Ourselves is in full effect.

3600

"Well, I think we're done here," Sonia says as she carefully stacks a bag of crunchy chocolate chip cookies atop our pile. And I'm about to answer her, except I'm holding a bag of sour cream and cheddar chips in my teeth. I already told you about this. You should know.

I admit it. This isn't my first snack rodeo. Yeah, Mom's the Snack Time Terminator, and WBD's all *health food's the best food yada yada nada*, buuuut they also both work full-time. Which means every Monday through Friday, outside of The Bronster, I'm all alone with *infinite time* to explore Snacktopia—scanning the pantry, scouting the kitchen cabinets high and low, foraging wherever Mom hides the best treats because she clearly doesn't trust me.

Which is totally unfair.

I take the bag out of my mouth and place it down on the counter. "Almost," I reply with a wink.

It's weird, how parents say one thing but practice another. Mom claims *junk food makes you sad*, yet we still keep a pretty decent-sized stash—especially when you know where to look. Mom's favorite stash spot's the top shelf in the pantry.

Which sucks if you're only 5′6″ like WBD and you need to use the step stool to reach the *second* shelf. I could understand if the very top shelf posed a problem, although my Real Dad, The Bronster, and Mom (if she really stretched out for it—Mom being extra bendable because of yoga and being double-jointed) could all get up there.

And fine, I use the step stool, too—but given our family's tall-people DNA, I'll hopefully ditch the stool by my fifteenth birthday. I mean, my Real Dad was 6′4″, so I'm not worried. But for now, I get on my tiptoes on the top step of the stool and reach into the way back of the pantry.

"Jackpot," I shout, hoisting the hidden can of spray cheese Mom had stashed there high above my head like a trophy.

3700

I lock the front door behind us. There's still daylight, the sun's a runny egg yolk, spilling across the sky. But night's starting to creep into the horizon, and if you stare east, you can see the frothy blue moonbeams swirling. I shift my bag of "essential supplies" to my other arm and check the bag swinging from Sonia's shoulder.

"You think the others made out as good as us at their houses?"

Sonia shrugs and a sparkly thing falls from her pocket and rolls along the sidewalk. I grab it and hand it back to Sonia. "You can't lose your coins. You worked hard for those."

She turns the gold token over in her hand. "Remember when we buried these coins all over the neighborhood and then got in so much trouble for digging up everybody's yards?"

"Umm, yeah. We lost like half the coins because somebody

drew way too many 'X marks the spots' all over our map!"

Sonia laughs. "Whatever. I told you, that was supposed to be grass!"

I crack up. "Who uses *X*'s to draw grass? Check marks maybe. I'll even give you *V*'s, but not *X*'s."

Sonia playfully hip-checks me off the sidewalk and into the grass. "Excuse me, but *somebody* kept hogging the black crayon that I needed for the *X*'s!"

"C'mon, there were like sixty-three other crayons to choose from."

Sonia grins. "You probably ate it."

I stop walking and throw up my hands. "For real, Sonia? I *knew* you were gonna take it there. Sheesh, a kid eats a yellow crayon *one* time in kindergarten and never lives it down."

Sonia holds up the peace sign. "*Two* crayons. You ate two. Yellow and green."

I shrug. "I thought they'd taste like lemon-lime."

Sonia throws her arm over my shoulders. "Well, I'm sorry, my friend, but I'm gonna be telling that story the rest of our lives, E."

Yep, Sonia's the only person on the planet who calls me *E*—and

I don't know, I sorta like that it's just something between us.

I roll my eyes. "Trust me, I already know. We'll be old and gray in the retirement home eating lunch and you'll still be telling that story."

"That's what friends are for," Sonia says and we both laugh.

And for a moment it feels like all is right in the world. Like this is a normal summer day. And we walk down the sidewalk a full block in perfect, easy silence—the way only best friends can. But then Sonia suddenly stops walking, which is weird because we're in the middle of the street.

"Hey, Eddie?"

"What's up?" I say, pausing beside her, our shadows stretching like giants across the pavement. She makes a weird face, like she's not even sure she should say whatever's on her brain.

"Isn't it kinda weird *none* of our parents have come back yet? The power's been out for hours now. And outside the five of us, we haven't even seen another human."

I nod slowly because, yeah, she's making very valid points, but also my gut tells me now's not the time to panic. That right now it's best if we keep calm and stick together.

"Well, it's not *not* weird," I admit, flashing her my *but everything's gonna be okay* smile because that's what a best friend does—

They help you get through the things that scare you, even when they're afraid, too.

But yeah, that thing about all the people not being here, I'm just gonna avoid that for now.

3800

The last time I saw this many snacks in one place, I was definitely at the grocery store. Seriously, we don't just have a mountain of snacks, guys—no, we have a whole mountain range! There are so many snacks that I *almost* feel guilty, like somehow just by visualizing all these sugary, salty treasures I've done something wrong.

Mom's not even here but her voice is *all up in* my head:

Eddie, don't you even think about eating all that junk food!

In fact, don't even look at it.

Eddie, I'm serious, turn your head! No, really, turn your head. I'm not playing.

Why aren't you turning your head, Eddie? You think I'm playing, don't you?

You better be glad I'm not there, otherwise I'd turn your head for you.

I don't care if everyone else is doing it. If they jump into a pond filled with bird poop, are you gonna jump, too?

Eddie, do you want a mouthful of cavities, is that what you want? Because that's what's coming. You're the one who's gonna have to sit in that dental chair with Dr. Miller's hands in your mouth while you try to explain how you got all those cavities.

Eddie, I'm not paying the dentist to keep your mouth healthy just so you can undo it all with this ridiculous snack binge!

Eddie, I know you're ignoring me. Wait until I see you next, Eddie Gordon Holloway. Ooooh, you're gonna get it.

And then things get weird because suddenly Mom's voice is softer, nicer, and she's laughing as if she's genuinely excited for me:

Eddie . . . Oh Eddie . . . Eddddiiiieeee, are you ready for the sugar rush of your dreams?

And once again I find myself in an embarrassing drooling situation.

"Eddie Gordon Holloway! Snap out of it!" a voice yells.

And snap out of it, I do. I shake my head so hard that a black hole opens up in my brain and then, *vrooosh*, it sucks all that

Mom Talk into its swirling vortex like a cosmic vacuum, before closing itself up again and vanishing in a blink. Which is when I realize everyone's looking at me weird, as if they're deciding whether to be concerned or commence howling away. Which, by the way, of the Nine Degrees of Laughter, howling's third best.

1. Closed-lip smile—perfect for when their joke's not funny but you don't wanna be rude. See: my reaction whenever WBD tries to be funny.
2. Chuckle (often sounds like *hehe*)
3. Giggle (you don't wanna laugh but you just can't help yourself)
4. Pig (a combo of snorting and squealing)
5. Guffaw (No, I'm not making it up, it's a real word!)
6. Chortle (Also, a real word! You guys really should read more!)
7. Howl
8. Drop to the ground in a fit of laughter
9. Your butt's off

"Let me guess, you just had a severe case of MOTB?" Trey asks.

My forehead slides up in confusion. "What's MOTB?"

Trey grins. "Mom on the Brain, a not-so-rare condition that leaves kids weak, dizzy, and paranoid."

And I can't help but laugh because, umm, nailed it. "I barely survived, guys. It was scary."

"It's okay. You're safe now," Sage assures me.

"Not just yet, he isn't," Trey says. "Because there's only one surefire way to beat *Mom on the Brain*."

"Oh yeah? And what's that?" I ask.

"You gotta do something super fun that your mom normally wouldn't approve of."

"Like what?"

Trey nods toward Snack Mountains. "That's a good place to start."

"If it's really the *only* way," I say, grinning as I survey the peaks and valleys of our snack horizon. "Except there's just one thing."

Trey's nose wrinkles. "What's that?"

"I can't do this alone," I say with a wink. "I'm gonna need some help."

"We've got your back," X says with a serious nod.

And what happens next is just like those movie action scenes they film in super slo-mo—

The five of us racing toward Snack Mountains, a look of utter determination on every one of our faces, pumping our arms, kicking our legs, running as fast as we can—

I'm not sure who leaps first, but all of us go airborne at nearly the same time, all of us smiling as we dive head- and foot-first into stacks of oatmeal chocolate chip cookies and individually wrapped servings of Fantastic Fudge Brownies, Peekaboo Popsicles, and Harry Larry Lemon Bars. Our five bodies crashing into mounds of rainbow-colored Tarties, piles of Grape and Strawberry Super Suckers, and heaps of shiny-wrapped Groober Toobers. We're laughing, creating a tidal wave of Very Cherry Really Wacky Waxy Lips and Very Berry Kinda Scary Bubble Burst Bolos, so many snacks flying in every direction as we smoosh our mountains into an ocean of Tooty Froot Fries, Banana Blossom Boomeroos, and Sweet and Sour Mellow Mallow Balls.

And no, none of us are at Beach Bash, but we're laughing, chasing each other across the lawn in our bare feet.

No, this isn't Beach Bash, but we turn licorice into fishing poles with neon gummy worms dangling on each line and we reel in Swedish Fish and candies shaped like barrels of root beer. And then when that gets old, we're back to chasing each other down the sidewalk, through our backyards—our fishing lines morphing into magic lassoes that we twirl above our heads like we're catching wild bulls.

And you're right, no one's mistaking this for Beach Bash but we're gobbling globs of goodies, stuffing and scarfing all the sweets we can eat, and washing it all down with still-cold cans of Porcupine Pineapple Soda—the extra-fizzy bubbles tickling our noses and throwing Sage into a burping frenzy, which makes us laugh harder.

And we're all tossing our heads back and conjuring the biggest belches we can burp and it's a contest, who can burp the loudest and the longest, and Sage wins easily, burping the entire alphabet in one continuous belch, which makes us laugh even more as we cheer her on, all of us impressed that the smallest and youngest person left us losers in her ABC burping dust.

And did I mention we're laughing?

"Best sugar rush ever!" I scream, tossing a brownie chunk into the air and catching it in my mouth, and everyone agrees.

"Best sugar rush ever!" they shout back. And when we can't possibly eat another fruity *this* or sour *that*, when our five sweet tooths are fully satisfied, a thing that before now we would've believed was entirely impossible because we were 100 percent sure you could never have *too much* of your favorite things, the five of us collapse into the grass on the shaded side of my house, lying on our backs with our arms and legs spread apart like we're making grass angels.

And okay, I know it sounds crazy but somehow the grass is softer, greener, lusher, the slender blades tickling our arms and legs, the breeze rippling over us. The sky's bluer now, too, and the clouds are closer, like if we really wanted we could reach out and pluck them down like cotton candy. Like, if we dared, we could leap into the clouds the way we leap onto our beds, feeling safe and happy as we slowly float away.

Yeah, this isn't Beach Bash, but it's a party.

It's *our* party. Our Party of Five.

And we're just getting started.

~~~

I reach into my pocket and remove a single blue pill, my afternoon dose of medicine. I toss it into my mouth and wash it down with a few chugs of bottled water.

"Umm, guys," Sage says, breaking the silence. "There's

something I forgot to tell you . . ." Her voice trails off in the wind.

I lift my head in her direction. Sonia sits all the way up, and X and Trey roll over onto their sides—four sets of eyes (five if you're one of those weird people who count glasses like they're another set of eyes).

"What's up?" I ask.

"What is it?" Sonia adds. "What's wrong, Sage?"

"It's . . . it's . . ." Sage wags her head slowly, her face twisted in horror as if she's seen a ghost. "It's . . . just . . ."

"Spit it out already, Sage, dang," Trey says. "What's the matter?"

"It's just this . . . *BURRRRRRRRRRPPPPPPPPPPPPPPPPPPP*. Whew, that one was stuck way down inside, ha. That felt great."

"Really, Sage? Is that really the thing you *forgot to tell us*?" X says, rolling his eyes.

"You scared the snacks outta us," I admit.

"Not cool, little sis," Trey says. "Not cool."

"You shouldn't play like that, Sage," Sonia chimes. "Now the next time you're actually in trouble, no one's gonna believe you."

Sage's whole face drops worse than the chocolate cake Mom baked last weekend, when she forgot to add baking powder, and the middle of the cake sagged like an old couch cushion. I mean, I still ate it anyway, but it was ugly.

"You guys, I was just joking. Man, I'm sorry. I thought it would be funny if I—"

But before she can finish her sentence, the four of us meet each other's eyes like *we got her*, and we officially reach "on the ground in fits of laughter" status.

"I hate you all," Sage says, grinning.

And then we're back on our feet, back to chasing each other down the block, back to laughing, back to having the time of our young lives, back, back, back.

And it feels like this day could go on forever, like the fun will never end—

But then the streetlights come on and we all freeze.

3900

"But how are the streetlights on if there's no power?" Sage asks.

Sonia shrugs. "The city must have them wired to some sort of emergency generator."

And you're all, *But Eddie, what's the deal with the streetlights?*

In a word: everything.

Because when you live smack-dab in the middle of Super Suburbia, USA, my friends, the funny thing is, streetlights are less about light and more about time management.

Let me break it down for you:

I told you I was basically given the freedom to do whatever I wanted all summer, provided I stay on top of my chores—but it's not like I was allowed to be out at all hours of the night.

No, during the day we can run around the neighborhood all day with our friends, playing ball, riding bikes, running down the ice cream truck dude only to be disappointed when you find out he only has lemon freezes left—you know, normal suburban stuff.

There's only one catch, though.

If you weren't home before those lights started shining, or better still, before they started warming up with that long, low buzzy hum they do, you were in for a world of parental pain.

Which is to say: Since the invention of time itself, streetlights have served as the official timekeeper for the sport that is *playing outside all day with your friends and not getting in trouble at the end of the day by your parents.*

Simply put: Always, always, always mind the streetlights.

Except now who was gonna yell at us to hurry up and get inside?

Usually this time of day you heard parents calling out their front doors, hollering across their yards—the screech of screen doors opening, the swoosh of patio doors gliding closed—as the stampede of young people returned to their respective homes.

But now?

There's nothing. Only silence. And who knew silence could be so loud?

4000

We're all sitting in a circle on my front lawn.

There's clearly something wrong with my ears, or my brain is somehow screwing up their words, because it almost sounds like . . . like they . . . but no, no, no, no . . . they can't possibly be actually considering . . . no way they'd actually . . . that would be . . . that would be . . . absurd . . . ha. No way. Noooo way. Of course not. Sheesh, get ahold of yourself, Eddie. Gosh.

It's just that for a second, I thought they were pretending like there's a possibility that our parents aren't coming home. Like we're competitors on *Super Survival* as opposed to, oh, I don't know, kids left alone on a cul-de-sac in northeast Ohio.

I scan their faces; surely at least one of them is smelling what I'm cooking. I mean Sage is basically a mind reader. You all saw it.

I save Sonia's eyes for last because of anyone, she's the person in this world who understands me most. I mean, seriously sometimes it's like she hears my heartbeat. It's almost scary.

Sonia smiles. "I know this is not what you want to hear right now."

See, what'd I tell you—scary.

"We should try to figure out how widespread the power outage is. Maybe search for a backup generator. Fill some coolers with ice to keep food stocked," Xavier says.

"All the coolers are at the *beach* along with all our friends and family and favorite slushies, so there goes *your* plan," I say.

"I'm sure we can find something well insulated to keep whatever provisions we—"

I promise I'm not Interrupt Everybody Guy—I *can't stand* that guy, always cutting you off mid-sentence as if whatever he has to say is smarter, cooler, or just flat-out more important. But I'm really getting annoyed now.

"Backup generator? Well insulated? First of all, it's just a power outage. Happens all the time, electricity will be back by tonight at the latest. I don't think we need to start putting together our apocalypse survival kits just yet."

"Okay, but suppose the power *doesn't* come back soon, then what?" Sonia asks.

"All I'm saying is better safe than sorry. Just think it's wise to think about our next steps if things don't go the way we want," Xavier says.

"This is half an idea like you have half a haircut," I say. "Did it come from the side of your brain where the hair isn't shaved?"

Point, Eddie. Plus a bonus for the solid haircut joke.

"Why are you so against this?" X asks, genuinely looking confused. "We all just went to get snacks from our houses and you were fine with that."

And yeah, maybe X just won a point back but we don't need to get into all that now.

"That was for fun. Part of the game. Snacks are temporary." And delicious, not to mention super comforting. "But this feels like a longer commitment."

I'm not the type to be afraid of commitment, you get me? If Ava Bustamante showed up right now and was like, *me and you, Eddie, ryde or die to the grave*, I'd be like, *Say less. I'm all the way in, with both feet.* But see, you can commit to an idea, too.

And I'm just saying if you're about to cuff up with one, you better be sure it's not a bad one. That you can live with it.

So first you test it out. Swish it around a bit, let your taste buds work out all the flavors.

Or, like my Real Dad used to say, *You gotta kick the tires.*

Gotta make certain it comes with a cash-back warranty.

"Eddie, we have to get prepared. We're on our own," X says. "We gotta start acting like it."

Okay, so he's just gonna . . . did he really just . . . so that's how it's going down . . . we just coming right out and saying the thing . . . wow. Quick, somebody call the cemetery because bro just killed the whole mood.

"What? Don't even say that. Who says that? Guys, help me out here," I say, pleading to the rest of the gang. But Trey shrugs, and surprise of all surprises, Sage actually stays quiet this time.

I turn to Sonia. She starts to say something but then Xavier shoots her a look and she stops herself—which is even more upsetting because Sonia and I are supposed to have each other's backs. And now she thinks it's a good idea to go searching for a *backup generator*—which I gotta be honest with you, I have zero idea what a backup generator even looks like. Seriously, it could be literally right next to me right now and it could say "Backup" and I would *still* have no clue what it was. And there wouldn't be any way for me to even explore it and try to figure out what it might be because anything that says "Backup" clearly doesn't wanna be messed with, amirite, hahaha.

Okay, so maybe in my head, I took a vote for the group on what everyone's role would be moving forward. Obvi, I'm the Leader, which sounds awesome I know, but trust me, it's a gift and a curse. And then Trey is the Muscle, because he's tall, super coordinated, and . . . muscly. Sage is the Negotiator because might as well put all that nonstop chatter to good use, amirite?! Sonia is the Brains because, well, she's probably smarter than all of us combined. And last but also least, Xavier is the guy with half a haircut.

"Now that that is settled, let's talk strategy," Sonia says.

Um, settled? Who said anything was settled?

But Sonia keeps going, completely ignoring my *oh for real* face. "Since none of us have a backup generator or some of the other stuff we need at our houses, we're going to have to expand the search around the neighborhood."

I shake my head. "Burglary. Your big genius plan is have us

robbing houses? In a blackout." And then I add, "I just don't see it." Because I can't help myself. I'm a sucker for a good dad joke. We've been over this.

"Oh, really?" Sonia says, with her *do you really wanna go there with me* eyes staring me down hard. "What about the robotic grasshopper?"

Wow. *Wow.* The gloves are definitely all the way off now.

And you're all, *Eddie, no way we're gonna let you gloss over the robotic grasshopper* . . .

Which, fine.

Long story short, I was four and I was at the store with Mom and this shiny thing that was hopping in the toy section caught my eye. I asked Mom if I could have it and she said she'd think about it. Except I forgot it was in my hands until Mom had already paid for her things and we were walking outside to our car. Mom saw it and made me go back in to return it. I tried to explain it was an honest mistake, but also, was it? It's hard to know what your four-year-old brain was thinking. Anyway, she made me apologize and I couldn't even get through it without crying crocodile tears and it was then that I made a promise to myself that I'd never again commit a single crime. A promise I have kept. And yet, as here I stand, my group of most trusted allies are asking me to join them for an evening of smash-and-grabs.

"I told you that story in confidence, Sonia."

Sonia frowns. "I know. But I'm just trying to get you to understand. We can't leave anything to chance right now, Eddie. We gotta do this. We don't have a choice."

And I start to argue *there's always a choice* but I look at the four of them, all of them just trying to do what they think is right, and I stop myself.

"We're borrowing this stuff, Eddie. When people get back, they'll understand. You think anyone is going to care that the kids who got left behind did what they needed to survive during a blackout?" Sonia asks, but in that way where she's really telling you what's good.

Trey points down the road. "Sage and I will start that way and we'll meet back here in an hour with what we find."

Everyone else nods.

So much for me being the leader.

4100

And it occurs to me for the first time—or at least, it's the first time I let the thought get all the way there. What if this is more than a game? A prank? What if we *never* figure out what this is, what's happened? And then it really hits me, like five knuckles to the face—I may never see my parents again. I'm an... orphan.

In just a few hours my entire life hasn't just flipped upside down, or inside out—suddenly, everything I thought I knew was now completely unrecognizable. There was nothing that I could cling to and no one, except Sonia, who knows me in all the same ways that I know them.

What if the way we're approaching any of this is all wrong?

What if this isn't just a temporary setback? What if this isn't just a new chapter, the next chapter, in the ongoing book of my life?

No, what if . . . what if this is an entirely *new* book?

4200

We split into two teams: Trey and Sage are Team A. Me, Sonia, and X are Team B. We agree to stick to the cul-de-sac for now. No sense wandering off too far, especially without knowing what's happening out there in the rest of the world.

I'm still not totally on board with the plan, but at the same time, I'm kind of interested about what's inside all these houses. You know when you go trick-or-treating on Halloween and everyone is all amped about getting to dress up or to get at that candy. I mean, I'm right there with them, of course. I like a full-size Snickers as much as anyone. But the extra, extra fun part of Halloween for me is that forty-five-second peek into your neighbor's house.

That bell gets rung and Mrs. Jackson down the way cracks her door just enough for you to see she's got a wall of Guaranteed to

226

Increase in Value over Time Collector's Plates or a shelf filled with like eighty tiny ceramic penguins. Some people really put the *strange* in stranger.

And what's up with Halloween, anyway? You know what I'm talking about. Your parents spend all these years telling you not to talk to strangers, and, nope definitely do not ever take candy from a stranger, so you don't. And then on this one day of the year, they're like, hey, go take this monster costume and pretend to be someone you're not, and go talk to all the strangers where *they* live, and take lots of candy from them.

Outside the first house, the Millers', I take a minute to make sure we're all really on board with this.

"How are we even going to get in here? Did you think of that part?" I ask.

X reaches down to this real-looking rock and picks it up and I'm thinking, *Oh so now we're smashing windows with rocks; this went too far too fast.*

Then the real rock slides open to reveal a key. You're fake, rock, I won't be forgetting that anytime soon. You think you know a rock and it turns out to be something totally different. Man.

Also, I told you X knows everyone all over the neighborhood. Of course he has a way in. That's probably been his plan all along.

"Shady," I say to X as he makes a big sweeping arm gesture like *after you* while the unlocked door swings open.

I've been inside some of my neighbors' houses before but it's a totally different animal without them watching, without them here to tell us what's okay to take and what's off-limits.

We decide to split up.

I call this floor, Sonia climbs the stairs to where the bedrooms are, and X draws the basement. "Why do I gotta go search in the dungeon?" he asks.

"Because we called the other floors, my friend," I explain. "You know how this works. You either call it or you don't."

"I didn't know we were calling out our choices."

"Right," Sonia says. "Because that's how call-its work. Someone kicks it off, in this case it was Eddie, and then the others jump in as fast as they can. And because I'm faster than you, I'm headed upstairs and you're hanging out in the basement. Don't be a sore loser, X."

"Whatever," X says. "You guys probably had the call-it already agreed on."

This is how things typically roll with us. The three of us are always together, but depending on the day and our moods and a host of other factors, whose side we were gonna take in our inevitable debates, arguments, and decisions changes all the time.

The day started with X and Sonia vs. Eddie but now it felt like I was getting some momentum back to the natural order of me and Sonia. I could hear X mumbling how unfair this whole thing was all the way down the steps. And don't tell him, because I'd hate for dude's head to get any bigger than it already is—especially given the current state of his haircut, it's best we not draw any more attention to his head than what is absolutely necessary—

Buuuut I love the guy. Yeah, we argue and crack on each other all day, and yes, our relationship is different from the ones we have with Sonia—but it's all love between us. I mean, we're brothers, no matter what. Even if he had me operating like a sneaky bandit in these trying times.

I work my way through the kitchen first. Open every drawer

and cabinet, including one that is literally five entire shelves of . . . wait for it . . . wait for it . . . prunes!

But not just regular ole prunes. No, this is five shelves of every prune form.

Dried prunes.

Canned prunes.

Prune juice.

Prune pie.

Prune tablets.

Prune candy.

I'm not one to judge, but it's kinda disturbing. I mean, there's only one of two explanations. Either the Millers have invested a lot of money in the prune business and are doing all they can to make sure prunes stay profitable, or . . . the more likely explanation, I'm guessing the Millers are having a serious problem with their regularity. I make a mental note to never open that cabinet again.

I find a few other odd things. A troll doll collection even though the Millers don't have kids. A box of sock puppets. A tin coffee can filled with double-A and triple-A batteries, most of which are corroded. There are good things to be had, too, though.

I find two flashlights, including one that works on solar power—which is a major score. And some beef jerky. Oh, and a huge bag of deodorant—which maybe doesn't seem all that important right now. But did you forget that I'm still shirtless and that it's beyond hot outside? Trust me, right about now, this bag of deodorant, it's basically like finding a gold nugget.

We work our way down the row of houses in the order that they come and every time, X finds a way in. He discovers the back door's unlocked. Or there's an extra key under the mat. Except at the De La Hoyas, all their doors are locked tight, and if there's a spare key hidden anywhere, we're never gonna find it.

"Welp, guess that's that," I say, already heading down the driveway toward the next house. But X is all, "Nah, bro, we gotta improvise." And the next thing I know he's shimmying up the gutter-pipe, sliding open a second-story window, and disappearing inside like a whole ninja.

I wait for him to poke his head out the window, tell me he's gonna let me in from the patio or something. But a few minutes pass and nothing.

"X, you okay?" I shout from the side yard but he doesn't answer me. I listen for any sounds of life but it's dead quiet. "I'm coming for you, X. Hold on, bro."

And just as I'm leaping onto the gutter pipe, doing my best to pull myself up—and okay, failing—I hear a noise at the front of the house. I race around and the door's wide open, X standing there chomping on a powdered donut, grinning like it's his birthday.

"Dude, I thought you fell down the stairs and were unconscious. I was trying to climb the house like you did to come save you."

"Aww, you *do* love me," X says.

I shrug. "I just didn't want anyone to find you with that messed-up haircut. No one should go out like that." Another point for me, ha!

But then X hurls a donut at my dome, igniting an explosion of powdered sugar on the side of my face, and okay, okay, two points for X, ugh, happy now?

Things we don't find at any of the houses we search: clothes that fit me! Except for the Jacksons. Their son is my size but his bedroom door was locked, and I don't know, it felt weird trying to bust inside a room that he clearly didn't want people in. I guess it gave me Bronster vibes.

"You sure you don't wanna knock the door down?" X says.

"It feels wrong to me."

X smiles. "Okay, but more wrong than you walking around in glorified boxer briefs?"

"Boys, are we playing nice?" Sonia calls from the other room.

"Forget nice," I shoot back. "We need to be playing barbershop with X's head. I keep hoping I stumble on some battery-operated clippers."

"Explain to me again why you thought it was a great idea to not do laundry the entire summer, my dude."

In the end, we come away with a lot of cool things, and more than a few random items. But no clothes for your boy. To be totally honest, I probably could have fit into something but I'm kind of liking this look. I feel free. What's the worst that could happen? A rainstorm? I mean, I'll be the first one dry ... I'm in a bathing suit! But I mean, I'm not about to tell them all that I'm feeling myself right now. That's a one-way ticket to Joke's-on-you-ville.

Also, no clippers to be found. But don't worry, like the short side of X's hair keeps saying to the tall, afro side—*Don't give up.*

You're gonna be okay. No, it definitely doesn't look that way right now, but I promise you, it's all gonna work out.

More than likely.

Probably.

Hopefully.

I mean, miracles happen all the time, right?

4300

When we get back to my yard we spend the next hour reviewing everything we collected. Sonia smartly suggested we inventory our supplies so that we knew what we had, that way if we needed to make another supply run, we wouldn't waste time or effort duplicating things we didn't need.

Sleeping bags, flashlights, batteries, pillows, Nerf guns, black licorice (yuck!), bottles of water, matches, pillows, a half-full bag of cat food because, according to Sage, *everyone knows cat food tastes way better than dog food.*

But now, inventory completed, we're just chilling in a circle of flashlights that Sonia and Trey organized on my front lawn. For real, it's like a fancy movie premiere from back in the day where they have all those big spotlights swinging circles of illumination around the ground.

"I think we need a couple more lights," X says, hopping to his feet. He walks over to our stack of supplies.

X grabs three more flashlights and clicks them on. I'm sitting in the grass directly across from him and for a moment his face is perfectly illuminated, and that's when I realize—

—my friend looks like a busted troll villain.

I mean, it's just *so* bad.

Apparently, I'm not the only one with X's hair on their mind because out of nowhere Trey says, "Hey, Xavier, I can fix up your haircut for you with scissors."

X shakes his head. "Thanks, man, but it's cool. I'll finish it when the power comes back."

"Why wait?" I ask.

X shrugs. "No offense, guys, but I'm not letting any of you people come anywhere near my hair."

"But Trey's really nice with scissors. He's as good as a professional barber," Sage says.

"No offense, but my hair is a unique texture that makes it harder to cut."

"I have a chain saw, too," Trey says, laughing.

"Can't you see he already tried that?" I say.

X rolls his eyes. "When are you gonna give your chest back to whatever bird you stole it from?"

Sage and Trey crack up. Meanwhile, Sonia does what she often does when X and I are going at it—she changes the subject. "Let's be real, this blackout really caught us all off guard," she says. "I was on level eighty-seven of *Monster Hunters II* when the power went out."

Xavier wags his head in disbelief, his eyes as wide as saucers. "I still can't believe you made it to the Hallowed Hunter Big Boss level."

"Your parents really let you play that much?" Sage asks.

"Are you kidding me?" I answer for Sonia. "Sonia's parents basically let her do anything she wants. In fact, I'm pretty sure they're the ones asking Sonia for permission to do things. I bet they asked you if they could go to Beach Bash today, didn't they?"

Sonia turns away before I can see her smile. "Yo, whatever, you don't know my life."

"Ohmigod, they really *did* ask you, didn't they?" Sage says.

"See what you did?" Sonia says, pretending to punch me in the arm. "Now you got these people thinking I'm spoiled."

I smile. "So, you mean, I've got them knowing the truth, then."

This time Sonia hits me for real and even though my instinct is to say *owww* I bite down on the quick burst of pain and it's gone as fast as it comes.

Listen, I'm not the type of dude who goes around saying stupid stuff like, *Wow, you punch hard for a girl.* This is partly because I was raised by an amazing mom who continues to make sure I don't say stupid stuff like that. But also because my best friend, Sonia, is an amazing human who will not tolerate such idiocy. So yeah, while I'm most definitely still very much prone to doing and saying things I regret, underestimating any of my fellow *Homo sapiens*? Yeah, that's not one of them.

"This whole thing is wild random, right? I'm not the only one who thinks that?" Trey asks.

"It makes about as much sense as X's half fro," I say with a smirk.

X sucks his teeth. "Dude, go put on a shirt. Oh, that's right, you literally don't have a single shred of clothing except for those cheesy pineapple swim trunks."

"I like his trunks," Sage says.

"Thank you, Sage. At least one person has taste around here."

"My little cousin Briana has the same pair," Sage finishes.

X can't stop laughing. "I'm sorry, is your face on fire from that knockout burn you just took from Sage?"

Okay, it was funny, even though I'm pretty sure Sage wasn't trying to burn me, but whatever. If you're gonna dish it, you better be ready to take it, Dad always said.

And then something weird happens. I look up and it's . . . nightfall. Like fully dark out, *finish dinner and homework, watch a couple TV shows, then go brush your teeth and get to bed* dark.

Sage yawns. "So we really sleeping outside?"

Trey nods. "You good with that?"

Sage tilts her head as if she's thinking it through. "Actually, I'm kinda . . ."

"Afraid?" I interject. "I'll be real. I'm kind of feeling a bit of that, too, right now. It just hit me all of a sudden. Like our families should be back now. Something's wrong."

Sage frowns. "I was gonna say I'm kinda excited to camp out, but I'm sorry you're afraid, Eddie. You can use my flashlight if you want."

"Awww, that's sweet of you, Sage," Sonia says.

"Yeah, thanks, Sage," I add. "So what, I'm the only one wondering what's happening?"

Trey shakes his head. "I mean, I think we all have lots of questions. Something's definitely happening. Something we don't understand."

"Okay, but like I know we're all sitting on our own theories, so let's hear 'em. What do you we think is really going on here?" Sonia pushes.

X bites his lip. "Well, we can rule out zombie apocalypse, seeing how I don't see any zombies staggering around."

"Okay, so if it's not zombies, then what else could it be?" Trey asks.

Sonia clears her throat. "Maybe everyone's been sucked into another dimension."

But I'm not buying this, either. "Okay, then, why didn't we get sucked into this inter-dimensional wormhole, too? Why are we still here?"

Sonia rolls her eyes at me. "Dude, we're just laying out theories, okay? That was mine."

I frown. "Isn't there a saying that states 'the simplest answer is usually the most likely answer'?"

Sage folds her arms. "Okay, so what's your simple answer, then?"

I shrug again. "I don't know. Maybe they all had car trouble." Everyone laughs at this idea, but I keep going, anyway. "Or maybe there was a big car accident and all the cars are wrecked. Or everyone got food poisoning and decided to sleep it off on the beach."

Sonia gives me her best "you've got to be kidding" face.

"Okay, maybe that's not what happened. But that's my point. We have no idea, and I just don't think it's helpful for us to stand around assuming the worst when we can't even confirm anything, okay?"

Trey gives me a half smile. "Eddie's right. Until we have reason to believe otherwise, let's just presume everyone's okay and instead focus our energy on holding down the fort until they come back."

X looks away. "Just saying, our family and friends wouldn't just not come back home unless . . . unless something awful happened."

Sonia nods. "Maybe not, but Eddie and Trey are right. Until we have more answers, our best play is to make sure we're prepared for whatever happens next, which means gathering all the supplies we can find."

"So what should we do first?" Sage asks.

"It's late now," X says. "And the last thing we need to be doing is stumbling around in the dark. But maybe tomorrow morning we consider launching a search party?"

"I'm good with that plan," Trey says. And we all echo the same. Even Mr. Bubbles barks his approval. He just appeared out of nowhere like he does and immediately cozies up with Sage in her sleeping bag, tickling her with his nose. If any creature knows how to thrive in times like these, it's this dog for sure.

And it's been decided: Tomorrow, we search for our families. And answers.

In the meantime, we all settle in for rest.

I can't tell you when I fall asleep, only that one minute I'm staring up at the open sky, at the constellations, at the moon, when I feel my eyes begin to droop. Sleep hitting me with the impact of a sledgehammer, dark, fast, and furious.

4400

I had the weirdest dream last night.

First of all, I missed Beach Bash because Mom made me stay home to do laundry. Ha! Can you even imagine how wild that would be? But the dream was even crazier—because on top of missing the festivities, the whole neighborhood lost power. But wait, there's more—everyone who went to the party disappeared! They never came back! And suddenly, it was just me and four other friends plotting out our survival in a world without our families.

Boy, am I glad to be in my own bed this morning.

I think that's what the dream was really about—

—making the most of things, no matter how tough your situation is. About keeping a great attitude, even in the face of the most challenging circumstances.

And I can't tell you enough how much I really—

Wait. Stop. Do you hear that?

Voices. Downstairs.

See, look, we're already putting the strange dream behind us. It's great to be awake. And best of all, the day has finally arrived! Today's the Bash!

I hop out of bed and race downstairs. Mom's talking to someone. I can't believe I'm going to say this but I'm even happy to see The Bronster and WBD.

But no—that doesn't sound like them.

The other person's voice is definitely familiar but I can't quite place it. I jump off the last two steps and slide into the kitchen.

I can't believe my eyes.

Seriously, I squint. I rub both eyes trying to make sure my vision's clear, and she's still sitting there at my family's kitchen island.

Yep, you guessed it. It's Ava B.

"Hey, Eddie, you're finally awake," Ava says. "My poor sleepy lil baby."

Wait, hold on, did Ava just call me her *baby*?

Mom moves some bacon around in a frying pan, wipes her

hands on her apron, and turns around toward me. "How come you didn't tell me Ava was such an amazing carpenter?" Mom asks.

My face scrunches. "An amazing what?"

Ava laughs. "I'm sorry, babe. I didn't know it was a secret."

And now I'm extra confused. "What are you even—"

But before I can finish, Ava hops up from the kitchen island and picks up a table saw from the ground—which is very odd and surprising, to say the least. Why is there a table saw?

And okay, why is Ava turning it on? And how is she turning this one two-by-four plank of wood into a massive bookshelf? And how is she gonna get that bookshelf out of the middle of our kitchen?

And wait, how is this bookshelf flying? I mean, it has wings shooting out its sides, I can clearly see that, but uh, how does it have wings?

I get that it's been a little weird around here and a lot of unexpected things have happened, but c'mon, bookshelves don't have wings. I'm 100 percent confident that bookshelves did not evolve to the top of the evolutionary chart, so what in the world is going on here?

"Hey, son," I hear a voice call behind me. "Thanks again for helping me work on the car last night."

I turn around and smile. "Oh, sure, no problem, Dad. Any time." I turn back around toward Mom and Ava, Dad slipping on his house shoes behind me.

Wait.

Dad.

Dad's here?

How is Dad here?

That's not possible.

"Of course it's possible, Eddie. I haven't been gone all that long, what, you already forgot me?" Dad asks.

"No, Dad, of course not. I'm so happy to see you. It's just that . . ."

"I'm sorry to interrupt but the bacon's jumping onto the ceiling again, honey," Mom says from the stove.

I look up and sure enough, five pieces of perfectly cooked bacon now stick to the ceiling, beads of bacon grease dropping onto my head. "Don't just stand there, silly," Ava says.

"Son, are you okay?" Dad asks. "Eddie, are you okay?"

But I can't talk. And I can't move. Because I'm very much not okay.

"Eddie, listen to me," Dad's saying. "I know this is all a lot to deal with, but you're a Holloway. You're built for this. You're ready. Everything's gonna be just fine, I promise."

But it's like the harder I try to say something, the more stuck the words are in my throat.

And then Dad's voice gets higher, screechier, like he's sucking on helium. "Eddie, Eddie, are you okay? Wake up, man! Eddie!"

Wake up? Huh? I'm already wide awake, how can I—

I feel a whoosh flow through my body like a shiver and suddenly my eyes pop open, and there's sweat running down my forehead. I'm lying down, yes, only I'm not in bed.

I'm not even in my house.

I'm not even indoors.

And there's someone leaning over me, shaking me, yelling at me to wake up.

"Sonia? What are you doing here?"

Sonia smiles. "That's what I was about to ask you, man. I didn't want to wake you up but it sounded like you might've been in the middle of a bad dream, so . . ."

I rub my head. "Where am I?"

Sonia helps me sit up. "In your yard, at our campsite. Did you forget? The world's going wrong? Our whole town's missing?"

Everything slowly comes back into focus. She's right, I am in a sleeping bag in the middle of my yard. Reality jolts me like an ice-cold shower.

It wasn't a dream—I *did* miss Beach Bash. It *is* only the five of us. Everyone *is* missing.

I'm *not* in a relationship with Ava.

And Dad's still . . . gone.

All of it a lie.

4500

Am I more than a little disappointed that today's picking up where last night left off before my awesome dream started? Of course.

But also, after I get into our wonderfully still-ginormous pile of snacks, I feel considerably better than when I first woke up.

"So, you wanna share your dream with us, or what?" Trey says, smiling.

I shrug. "There's not much to share. I barely remember it." Okay, that's a lie. But seriously, I'd rather not discuss that I thought my dad was here and that Ava B. was crafting five-shelf oak bookcases in the middle of my kitchen because . . .

That's a lot, even for me.

Sage grins. "All I know is you kept saying, *Ava, you're so good with a saw. Do you make dressers, too?*"

And everyone laughs, including me.

X mimics a high-pitched voice, "Oh Ava, make me a bench."

"Respect the woodworking game," I say, still smiling.

"So, what should we do about the bathroom situation?" X poses to the group.

"What do you mean?" Sonia says.

"We don't have power," X says. "How are we supposed to flush without power? Without running water?"

All of us frown but it's Sage who breaks the news to X. "Dude, running water doesn't need electricity."

"You've gone to the bathroom like six or seven times since the power went out," I say. "Have you not been flushing?"

And if you ever wondered if Black people blush, one look at X's face right now and you have your answer. "Huh? What? Ha. I was just . . . I was just playing with y'all. Hahaha. I really, uh, I had you going, didn't I? You really thought I didn't know that power and water don't have anything to do with each other? I mean, even Sage knew that and she's only ten."

"Nine," Sage says, patting X on his arm. "And it's cool, man. No one knows everything. That's why we're better together."

X smiles, his embarrassment level quickly dropping. "Thanks, Sage. And also I didn't mean anything by the age comment."

Sage shrugs. "Age ain't nothing but a number, my man."

"Well, I should, uh, probably go flush some … things … down …" X says, slowly backing away from us. "At least water is one less thing for us to worry about."

"If only we could say the same about your hair," I say. "Is it just me or did the uncut half grow another three or four inches overnight?"

X pretends to laugh. "Haha, very funny."

"Whatever," I snap back. "Don't you have a few toilets to flush?"

He rubs his stomach. "There's only one that's really gross and that's the one I left in your house, so it's all good."

And okay, this is the part when I chase him around the outside of the house.

I can't deny that he's definitely brought his A game. Meanwhile, me—at least when it comes to Olympic sprints around my yard—I'm at more like my B game.

As in my breakfast game.

X looks over his shoulder as I collapse onto the grass and he smiles. "You'd think you'd be faster than me, considering you're basically naked."

I turn my head toward him. "I'm *not* naked."

"I know I've asked you multiple times now, but humor me again, why is it exactly that you *still* rocking these swim trunks and nothing else? I mean, you think it's hard looking at my hair, try having your weird belly button staring at you, see how you feel then."

"Daaaang, he's killing you today, Eddie," Sage says, busting out laughing.

And I would definitely go in on him, guys, but to be real, I'm a little short of breath at the moment. "You better be glad I ate all those snacks," I say. "It's really slowing me down."

Xavier rolls his eyes and smiles. "So, is that a no to the part where you go find some actual clothing?"

"Depends," I say, spitting out a blade of grass. "Is this the part where you stop mistreating half of your hairline? Seriously, bro, your head looks like a bar graph."

"He's baaaaack," Sonia sings.

We all roll in the grass, the sun shining down on us. Maybe I'm crazy but I think Dream Dad was right. Everything's gonna be fine.

4600

I'm not sure how it happens but in the late morning we all sorta fall into our own rhythms. I suppose it makes sense that we'd want and need some alone time, after spending the last full day Velcroed to each other's sides.

Sonia's sitting on the deck in Mom's favorite Adirondack chair, her nose buried in a book. Every minute or so she pushes her glasses up on her nose.

Sage is sitting twenty yards away, her back to us as she leans against the base of a tree, doodling in her sketchbook.

I can hear the soft purr of a good nap as X catches a few zzzz's atop his sleeping bag.

Trey, not even an arm's length away, lies on his back, staring up at the sky. It's weird, because while there have been flashes of confident, super-awesome Trey—the guy everyone loves and admires—he's still not the same kid.

I get that none of us are after all that's happened since yesterday, but even before things started getting serious—when we still expected our parents and families to come home any minute—he just wasn't himself.

I don't get a chance to continue my thoughts, because suddenly my pocket's buzzing like crazy.

What in the world's going on? I think as I slide my hand into the pocket of my bathing suit. That's when I realize what's happening. The source of the vibrations.

It's my phone.

Someone's calling me!

4700

Except I can't get my phone out of my pocket. I'm obviously too excited, sure, but also the dumb angle I'm sitting in makes it way harder than it needs to be.

I'm fumbling around, rolling onto my side, trying to get it out.

It's only a few seconds but it feels like forever.

My phone was losing battery fast yesterday. I didn't even think it would still be charged.

Then I manage to finally get it through the opening and out of my pocket.

My eyes sweep across the various spots in the yard to see if anyone else has noticed this new development. But also to make sure nobody has seen me flopping around like a dying fish out on land.

At first I think *no*, that I'm alone in this moment. But then Trey's eyes meet mine and he mouths, "What's up?"

Before I reply his eyes follow my hand and zero in on my phone and he rolls even closer.

"Who is it?" he asks. "Answer it, answer it."

I'm nervous as I lift it up to my face, I won't lie, because what if this is the info we've been waiting for? What if I answer it and I hear Mom's voice? And she's crying because she hasn't been able to reach me for a full day—which is like a thousand years in mom time?

It hits me that I'll never hear my dad's voice again and, at this point, I may never hear my mom's voice again.

What if this is the call that validates our worst fears: that we are indeed alone, together?

That there will be no tearful reunions with loved ones.

No Beach Bash Part II held to celebrate everyone's safe return.

"Answer it already!"

I don't even look at the screen, because I can't bear to, because there's no time.

"Hello?" I say. "Hello?"

4800

"Who is it?" Trey whispers to me so as to not alert the others. "What are they saying?'

I shake my head. "They're not saying anything. It's just . . . silence."

He reaches out for the phone and I hand it to him.

He doesn't even have it two seconds when his face drops. "Bro, there was no phone call."

"What do you mean?"

He holds the dim screen at an angle I can see: 7 percent charged. And okay, I feel eighty-seven levels of idiot because he's right. No one was calling me. "It was just your alarm, man. Sheesh. Way to lift and dash a kid's hopes in a matter of seconds."

I frown. "I'm so sorry."

Trey shrugs. "It's okay. I'm just glad Sage wasn't here to hear it. Hate for her to get her hopes up too high, you know?"

I nod. "It's awesome how you two take care of each other."

Trey clears his throat. "Yeah, well, even though she talks way too much, and generally annoys me, she's a pretty great little sister." He shoots me a look. "But if you tell her I said that, I'll deny it and tell Sonia and X that you thought your alarm was a phone call."

I laugh. "I'll take that deal." And we bump fists to make our pact official.

I know you guys are probably gonna roll your eyes and call me corny, but if you would've told me that there was any situation on any planet in my entire lifetime that would include a moment where I was lying on my back shoulder-to-shoulder with the most popular, most athletic kid in our school, and probably in our entire school district, and that we'd be almost kinda sorta . . . friends—I'd never have believed you.

I get hyped just thinking about it. What if everything goes back to normal and Trey becomes this big, famous athlete? And because of today, we're like best friends forever. I get to be part of his crew, and when he needs business advice, he only trusts me because we slept out on my lawn together that day the lights went out. And because he's Trey, he's not just going to be a regular athlete, he's going to have a lot of companies and I'm going to run his production studio and get every pair of sneakers he ever puts out. And maybe one day, he does a series of interviews in a barbershop and I get to be in them and we talk about how bad X's haircut was for an hour on cable television.

Maybe it could happen; I mean nothing about the last twenty-four hours is very believable, and here we are.

"So, what's it for?" Trey asks.

"What's what for?"

He chuckles. "Your alarm, man. Why'd you set it?"

"Oh," I hear myself say, because for a split second I don't know why I set it. But then, in an instant, it all comes flooding back.

I can't even believe I almost forgot.

4900

I insert the key and unlock the door with Trey on my heels.

I head for the kitchen, open the cabinet I open every day, twice a day, and grab my prescription bottle.

Trey hands me a glass he's filled with water.

"Thanks, man."

He nods. "I suck at taking pills. They always get stuck in the back of my throat."

"Next time take it with a spoonful of applesauce or yogurt. Goes down like a dream."

"I'll try that," Trey says. "Have you always taken medicine for your . . . ?"

"My ADHD," I say with a smile. "It's all good, man. I'm not embarrassed to talk about it. You don't have to be, either. And the answer to your question is no, I've been taking medicine for almost two years now. We tried lots of other things first. I'm lucky, my doctor's pretty awesome. She's really helped me understand how to put myself in the best position to succeed. It's a process, you know, and some days it's harder to manage, but for the most part, I'm in a good place. Helps that my family's always been supportive. Even The Bronster."

Trey's nose wrinkles. "The who?"

I laugh. "Sorry. I mean my brother."

Trey nods. "Yeah, I know him."

"Not like I do," I say with a shrug.

Trey looks serious, though. "People ever give you a hard time for taking medicine?"

I shake my head. "No one that matters. I don't care what anyone else thinks. I'm just trying to be the best version of myself, same as everyone else, you know?"

Trey nods, stabs his hand in his pocket, and pulls out something blue and plastic.

"You have . . ."

"Asthma," he says. "Yep. Since I was a kid."

"But you're such a freak athlete. Dude, you dominate every sport. Even track. Your hundred-meter times are insane!"

Trey laughs. "Well, thanks. I appreciate your support."

I feel my face warm a bit. "Sorry, I didn't mean to be over the top about it."

"No, no, you weren't. It's just strange sometimes, how excited people get when they talk about me and that stuff. It's hard to explain."

"I can't even imagine the pressure you must feel."

He shrugs and I can feel the words coming—he's gonna say, *Nah, it's no big deal.* The words on the tip of his tongue. "It's not a big deal," he says.

Told you, guys.

"I doubt that's true," I reply.

His face falls and he turns away. My heart plunges because I've said the wrong thing. I messed up and now, not only are we not gonna be friends, Trey probably regrets telling me anything. I can't believe I blew it. I was only trying to give him the space to be his *completely authentic self*—like what Dr. Liz says. I wanted to give him whatever room he needed to be honest about how he actually feels but I pushed too hard.

"I didn't mean it in a bad way," I add on. "I know this is probably weird to say, but it just occurred to me that maybe you don't get to complain very much. That maybe people are so used to seeing you succeed in everything you do, you don't get to say you're afraid, you don't get to ask for help. Failure's not an option for you." I pause, wanting him to stop me from rambling, but he stays quiet, so I do what I always do whenever I'm unsure what to do—I keep talking, ha. "I'm not some amazing athlete, and obviously I don't have the pressure of the world on my shoulders, so I'm not pretending to know how you feel. It's just that . . ."

"Don't," he says, his back still to me.

"Don't what?"

"Don't do *that*. Don't sell yourself short just because you don't play basketball or find twenty notes stuffed in your locker with people asking to be your friend or telling you how much they like you . . ."

"Whoa, is that for real? Like you really get notes like that?"

He swivels back to me and holds his stare for what feels like ten minutes—although, it's probably not even ten seconds. "Sometimes . . ." he starts. "Sometimes the pressure feels like it might snap me in half."

I'm really regretting what I was thinking about Trey out on

the lawn. I'm sure everyone wants something from him all the time. And I was no different. Of course he can feel that. I don't know why I find that so surprising. He's a human being; he gets nervous and anxious. Of course he's afraid of failing.

I don't reply right away. Not because I don't want to, but because I want to say the right thing. Whatever's happening in my kitchen right now, whatever this moment is that we're having, I know that it's one of those important conversations—where you walked away feeling seen, understood, and validated. Where a friendship based on trust and respect is cemented.

"That must suck," I say—which admittedly sounded a lot better in my head, ugh.

But Trey laughs. "It sucks so bad," he says, nodding. "I hate it, man."

And I remember one of Dr. Liz's favorite pieces of advice to me and I know she'd want me to pass it on. "We need to first admit to ourselves that we don't like a thing or situation before we can start the work of changing it."

"Wow, that's kinda deep, Eddie."

"My therapist said it. She's the deep one."

"I like how you're so open about stuff. Like your . . . ADHD.

And your medicine. And therapy. I feel like people usually try to hide the stuff they're not sure people will accept."

I shrug. "I'm lucky. Seeing a therapist is a privilege a lot of people don't have. And having parents who've always given me permission to be myself, even when that meant doing or saying something that they wouldn't have, I'm lucky that way, too."

"You gotta start giving yourself more credit, man."

I throw up my hands in surrender. "Okay, okay, you're right. I'll try."

"Yeah, you will. Because I'm gonna stay on your butt and make sure of it."

And we bump fists again, exit the kitchen, and walk toward the front door.

"Hey, Eddie. One more thing?"

"Yeah?"

"On a scale of one to ten how mad were you when I missed that shot?"

"What shot?"

His eyebrows slide up. "Bro, you were there, I saw you. The shot that would've won the championship."

"You did win the championship," I say. What shot is he talking about? Did Trey have a dream where our team didn't win it all this year? I'm so confused.

"I didn't. Reggie Conroe got the rebound and hit the game winner. If he didn't, we would've lost on my shot."

That's what Trey's been carrying this whole time? A shot he didn't hit that didn't matter anyway?

"Honestly, when I think about that game, I don't even remember the shot you didn't make. You had nineteen points, four assists, and five rebounds. Without you, we wouldn't have even been in the game. We wouldn't even have had a season!"

"Dang, you remember my stats?"

"Umm, duh. You were putting in work out there, man. And that's my point. If you weren't on the team, do you have any idea how awful we'd be? Like we'd be lucky to win a single game."

Trey laughs. "The team's not that bad, c'mon."

I shoot him a look and now it's his turn to surrender.

"My dad was super competitive, and he was a great athlete. Honestly, he was great at everything he did. I never thought about it until now, but I'm guessing he probably had some of the same pressure and expectations as you."

"Your dad's a legend. He's all over the trophy case at the high school," Trey says.

I can't believe he knows Dad from his records although I shouldn't be surprised since Trey probably broke half of them.

"He was a born winner. But he was an even better dad. His job was tough, he had to work a lot of hours, but he promised me he'd always be home before I went to bed, that no matter what, him and me would always talk every day. And man, he was hilarious. The funniest human ever. He'd have you rolling on the ground feeling like you were gonna throw up, that's how hard he'd make you laugh."

"Wow, he sounds awesome. That's gotta be hard, him not being here. You miss him a lot? Sorry, that's a stupid question."

I wipe my eyes because for some reason they're starting to water—probably allergies. "I miss him so bad it hurts."

"I'm sorry, Eddie."

"But wait, get this. Can you believe he sometimes overslept and made me super late for school, even though he knew how much I hated not being on time?"

Trey shrugs. "I'm sure he didn't do it on purpose."

"He also had the worst morning breath ever. Oh, and he once

slammed my elbow in the car door. And he missed my fourth-grade choir solo because he had to travel for work."

Trey waves his hands. "Whoa, dude, what's happening here? Why are you talking junk about your dad? Of course he wasn't perfect. He made mistakes. But you said so yourself, he was a great dad. He tried hard. He loved you. And that's how you should remember . . . him . . ."

A smile slowly spreads across his face. "Ohhhh, I see what you did there. You're saying in the end we're not defined by our mistakes or failures. The people who love us and believe in us, the people we love and believe in back, don't care that we missed the game-winning shot. They just care about us. Who we are inside." And now he's really grinning. "Pretty smooth, Eddie Holloway."

I wink at him and nudge his arm with mine. "I have no idea what you're talking about, big man. That was all you."

5000

You're all, *Oh snap, Eddie, what a terrifically touching—and super-sappy—moment.*

Seriously, the only way that could've gotten any sappier is if it were in the middle of the forest.

Which, wow, guys, wait to hit me with a perfectly timed dad joke, ha. I love it.

But also, don't worry, because the second Trey and I step outside, everything immediately goes bad.

I pull out my keys to lock the door behind us and Trey looks at me kind of weird, like, *We're the only ones here. Why are you bothering to lock the door?* I mean, we're literally living on the front lawn these days. But still, I can't help but hope somewhere in my heart that Mom will still show up back here. And if she came home, to her house, where she lives, and I'd left the door unlocked, well, let's just say all that mom relief of me being okay would be quickly replaced with mom anger and mom responsibility-for-your-actions.

I get the lock handled and I'm about to put the key back in my pocket when something crashes into my legs, knocking me to the ground.

"Hey, easy, Mr. Bubbles," Trey says, extending me a hand to help me back on my feet. "You okay, Eddie?"

I brush myself off and turn to Mr. Bubbles. "I'm cool. Not the first time I was attacked by an aggressively friendly dog." I reach for my house key, my fingers nearly around the lanyard when it happens. "What are you doing? Hey, come back here, Mr. Bubbles!"

Yep, Mr. Bubbles steals my keys.

Which I realize isn't anywhere near the worst thing that could happen, except without that key I can't get back inside the house. And if I can't get back inside, I can't take my medicine. Which means—

I start running as fast as I can after Carterville community's favorite canine. But not only does he have a great head start, he's also just way faster than me as he practically gallops down the road like he's a horse in the Kentucky Derby. What can I say—I'm smart and funny, and dare I say charming, but in the speed department, I'm pretty average.

Fortunately, I have friends to help.

Sage drops her sketch pad and takes off after Mr. Bubbles. Sonia abandons her book and joins in, too. Even X wakes up long enough to ask what's going on before immediately falling back to sleep, the drool pool getting bigger and bigger between his face and sleeping bag.

We try to corral him.

We try getting ahead of him.

We try boxing him in and forcing him to run into one of us.

But in the end, none of us can even keep up with him. Mr. Bubbles is juking us left and right like an NFL running back.

Which means, I'm gonna have to break into the house to get my medicine. I think about which window makes the most sense to break, which one Mom would be less upset about, the answer being the one on the top floor of nowhere, ever. Mom would never not be mad about me breaking a window, even though it's not my fault the neighborhood dog's a thief and did this to me.

But then just as me and Sonia and Sage are forced to give up our chase, something magical happens. Trey appears out of nowhere, sprinting as if he's on fire and Mr. Bubbles is the cold pond he needs to extinguish his flames.

Trey does what only the most special of athletes can do: He kicks things up a notch, throwing himself into high gear and leaving the three of us to gawk in admiration, amazement ... and, okay, maybe a pinch of jealousy, too, because dang, dude has Superman speed.

"Well, folks, you wanted the race of the century, and boy, are we getting that today," I say in my best sports anchor voice. "Mr. Bubbles, the early favorite, got off to an incredibly fast start down the straightaway of the cul-de-sac, easily lapping the entire field and appearing set to cruise to victory. Well, almost the entire field."

Sonia smiles at me. "That's right, Edster. Almost. Because what our sneaky canine companion didn't count on was a special appearance by Carterville County's best athlete in the last decade, Trey Davis."

"You're right about that, Sonia. I'm watching it with my own eyes, guys, and it still doesn't feel real. Trey Davis is beyond gifted. A generational talent," I add.

"Trey, you got this, big bro. Mr. Bubbles, you're going down!" Sage shouts, using her cupped hands as a megaphone.

"Looks like his coach and sister's yelling some words of encouragement. That's gotta feel good, Edster, having your flesh and blood in your corner like that."

"You betcha, Sonia. My goodness, did you see that? Trey Davis just hurdled an entire row of shrubbery. That must've been five feet tall and five feet wide, but who knows, I struggled with geometry, so."

"Yeah, you did. But I'll tell you who's *not* struggling, Edster. Trey 'All-American' Davis. He scaled that fence effortlessly and now he's closed the gap separating him and the pack leader, Mr. Bubbles, another two feet. The only question is, will he be able to sustain this kind of speed?"

"No doubt, Sonia. In fact, I'm pretty sure he's got a whole other gear he could ratchet up to, if need be. I tell you, I'm just so impressed by this kid. He's a hard worker and by all accounts a great human."

"Wow, Mr. Bubbles is showing zero signs of quitting out there. He's the ultimate competitor. The last thing he'd do is disrespect the game by giving it anything less than his all."

Mr. Bubbles doubles back around and heads down the driveway of the Walsh house.

"No truer words, Sonia. My oh my, Mr. Bubbles is really giving Trey fits now, as he knocks over half a dozen trash cans. Mr. Bubbles is doing anything he can to slow his pursuer down."

"But what's this? Did that really just happen, partner, or are my old eyes playing tricks on me?"

"Normally, I'd say it was your eyes, except this time I saw it, too. Trey Davis barreled through those barrels like they were nothing."

"And by barrels, he means trash cans, folks."

I shoot Sonia a look. "I said what I said."

"Wait a minute, I think Mr. Bubbles's strategy is starting to reveal itself. During this entire race, I wasn't sure about his game plan, but now I think it's getting clearer."

"Huh? You don't think he's headed for—"

"The sewer grate? I'd say he's definitely headed there."

We run to catch up because that's the one place we can't let him beat us to—if he drops my keys down there, you can kiss those babies goodbye for good. There's no way we're fishing them out.

"Trey," I yell. "He's headed for the sewer at the end of the street."

"Looks like Trey Davis is unfortunately running out of time. If he's gonna have any hope of catching Mr. Bubbles, he's gonna have to make his move soon, before it's too late."

"But wait, what's happening? It appears Trey Davis is turning right, leaving Mr. Bubbles alone with a clear path. This is certainly a surprising development, Sonia." C'mon, Trey, what's going on?

"It looks like Trey's eaten enough of Mr. Bubble's doggy dust to last him a lifetime, and he's packing it in. Even still, what a valiant effort by that young man. He should hold his head high."

We run down the street faster, but still not quite fast enough to catch Mr. Bubbles—and then we see it. A collection of chewed-up tennis balls, lying on top of the grate. It's about to be all over. In a few seconds Mr. Bubbles will get there, drop my keys on his stash spot, and probably pick up one of his tennis balls. The balls rest on top of the holes but my keys are too small. They'll fall through and will soon be at the bottom of the sewer.

"Sorry, man. We'll figure out a way to get inside your house," Sonia promises as we slow down to watch the conclusion of Mr. Bubbles's one-dog play.

"It's all over, folks. Mr. Bubbles must be feeling pretty good about this victory right now," I say. "But also, he better not ask me for anything today because I am not a fan in this moment."

"And Mr. Bubbles leaps into the air; he's mere seconds away from his target. Wow, talk about unexpected—wait, hold the phones, do you see that?"

My eyes follow where Sonia's pointing. "See what?"

"There's something zipping along from out of Mr. Arnold's backyard."

That's when I see it.

Trey cut through a backyard and is now running right at Mr. Bubbles from the side.

"OMG, folks, that's Trey Davis. Did he really just outsmart us all?"

"I think he did. I think that's exactly what he did."

"Go, Trey. Go, Trey, you got this!" Sage says, pumping her fists in the air.

"He's not gonna make it," Sonia says.

"It's gonna be close," I say.

And we all watch in utter disbelief as Trey Davis leaps into the air—

Mr. Bubbles is somehow *still* airborne and the two of them are headed right for each other.

"Who's gonna win? Who's gonna grind it out?" Sonia says.

"My money's on Mr. Davis," I say.

And it turns out to be a wise investment as Trey meets Mr. Bubbles in the air, his hand reaching for my lanyard dangling from Mr. Bubbles's canine chompers, before the two of them crash hard onto the ground.

"Treyyyyy!" Sage screams, running up the rest of the block.

Sonia stops her. "Wait, Sage, give him a second. I see something."

Trey is rolling on the ground away from the sewer grate. He's on his back, then on his front, then on his back again.

Finally, he stops a few feet away from where he started.

There's nothing but silence.

"Anybody lose a key?" Trey asks, grinning and wiping the dirt from his eyes with one hand and holding up my lanyard in his other.

"Miracle of miracles, Trey Davis does it again," I say. "This guy's special."

"Understatement of the year, Edster," Sonia says. "A bravura performance for the ages."

"Now *that's* a game winner!" I say loud enough for Trey to hear.

"Hey, there you guys are," a sleepy voice behind us says. X pulls his bike up beside us. "So, what'd I miss?"

5100

I can't say what sparks us.

Maybe it's Trey's heroics.

Or how hard we laughed when X showed up after missing the whole thing.

We had jokes about him sleeping through the most epic display of athleticism this block has ever seen on the whole walk back to my yard.

Maybe it's because we realize that we're more resilient, more adaptable than what we gave ourselves credit for. Sure, there's still a few things to work out, like the power thing. And yeah, it becomes clear to us that as much as we complained about our parents, about our families, having them around definitely made life a lot easier.

I mean, The Bronster is as annoying as siblings come but I can say, having him around kept things . . . interesting, ha. There was never a dull moment.

Not that we're having many of those ourselves.

I guess it's just that moment when you realize how much you took for granted—and how you'd do almost anything to have it back. As much as I want to see Mom, and wouldn't mind seeing The Bronster, I admit, even WBD's face would be a welcome sight right about now.

We pass a giant jar of peanut butter around, each of us already with slices of bread in our hands.

"I miss Mom and Dad," Sage says, sucking a glob of peanut butter off her thumb. "Is that weird?"

Trey wraps his arm around his sister's shoulders. "No way. I totally miss them, too."

"I hate how quiet it is now. Between all the empty houses and the lack of power, I feel like I can hear ants marching through the grass," Sonia says.

"I know we already discussed it, but I keep thinking, maybe we should go check things out on the beach," X says.

I can't pretend I haven't given that idea more thought, except the problem is . . .

"You do realize we're not gonna go there and find our families, right? Like they're not still partying on the beach or whatever," I say.

"I know that, but what else are we gonna do? Just sit here and wait for something to happen? How's that better?"

Sonia shrugs. "It's safer."

Sage nods as she takes a big giant bite of her sandwich. "But you can't win when you play it safe."

Sage and Trey fist-bump. "That's my sister," Trey says, grinning. "Go big or go home, that's what I say."

There's a part of me that knows whatever we find out there, if we find anything, isn't likely to be good. Whatever happened to everyone is bad enough that we all got left here alone overnight. Except Mom wouldn't do that on purpose. Not if she could help it. Not in a million years. And I'm pretty sure the other families feel the same.

If they were in danger, or hurt, and there was a way we could help them, well, wasn't that worth every risk?

"Take a vote?" I suggest and everyone nods. "All in favor of going to the beach?" Everyone raises their hand. "Well, that was easy."

"So when's this search expedition going down?" X asks.

Trey shrugs. "First thing in the morning?"

"How about after lunch?" I ask and the four of them look at me like, *What's gotten into you?*

I smile. "Hey, go big or go home, right? If we're gonna do this thing, we probably shouldn't waste any more time."

Sonia breaks off a piece of her crust and nods. "I second the motion."

"Oh yeah!" Sage grins, her teeth covered in peanut butter. "We're going on a mission!"

"Just one question," Trey says. "How are we gonna get there?"

"Our bikes?" Sage offers.

"It's way too far to pedal," X says.

"It would take almost a whole day, best-case scenario," Sonia agrees. "And it's like Eddie said, time's not something we wanna waste right now."

"Don't the Connors have those electric scooters?" X suggests, before immediately slapping his forehead. "Oh, right, we don't have power."

I nod. "And even if we did, there's only two scooters."

"Two of us could go and check things out, then report back?" Sonia says.

"I think it's best we stick together. The last thing we wanna do is lose each other," Trey says. And we all mumble our agreement.

X frowns. "Okay, so then how are we getting to the other side of town before dark?"

And it hits me like a lightning bolt. "Guys, I have a plan!"

Everyone groans, but because I'm feeling good right now, I choose to interpret their whining as positive words of support.

Besides, it's like Sage said, we've got a mission to execute.

"Meet me in front of my house in ten minutes," I tell everyone as I chow down on the last bite of my sandwich and pop to my feet.

"You're not gonna tell us this brilliant plan of yours?" X asks.

But I'm already jogging toward my front door.

"Wait, where are you going?" Sonia calls after me.

But I keep running. "Ten minutes! Don't be late!"

5200

"Okay, so Eddie tells us not to be late, but then he's late. Figures!" I hear X complain as he and the others wait for me in my driveway. Except I'm not late. In fact, I'm right on time.

I tap the garage door opener and nothing happens.

"Oh, duh," I say out loud.

I squeeze my way to the door and open the garage door the old-fashioned way—

With my muscles, ha!

The garage door slowly lifts, and there are my four friends, who just very well may be four of the last people on earth—I mean, who knows what's happened to the rest of the world, right?

They all squint in the bright sunlight, but not me, because I've got my shades on.

"Um, Eddie, why'd you open the garage?" Trey asks as I slide into the front seat, glide my fingers across its buttery smooth leather. Okay, so maybe I see now why WBD's so crazy about this car. It *is* beautiful.

"Wait, where did he go?" Sage says. "This sun is doing too much right now."

I smile to myself. *You sure about this, Eddie?* you guys ask. And I appreciate your concern, I do—but I've never been more certain of anything in my life.

I turn the key and the engine roars to life, and in the rear-view mirror I see the four of them nearly jump outta their skin.

X shields his eyes with his hand, trying to peer into the car. "Eddie, are you crazy?"

I throw the car in reverse, and slowly take my foot off the brake, and the car begins rolling backward. I honk the horn to clear the path. "Move it or lose it, guys!" I yell out the open car window.

Thirty seconds later, Sonia's sitting next to me in the front passenger seat, Trey and Sage holding down the back seat. But where's X, you ask?

X is folding his arms and tapping his foot in my driveway. "Nuh-uh, no way I'm getting in the car with Eddie driving. Are you kidding me? You guys must have a death wish. But not this guy. Nope. No way. Besides, how come Trey isn't driving? He's the oldest."

"Um, no way I'm driving Eddie's stepdad's car, sorry," Trey says, waving X off.

Sonia rolls down her window. "X, get in the car, man."

But X only refuses even more, louder and more stubborn by the second. "Um, it wasn't that long ago Eddie wouldn't even let me peek under the protective covering and now suddenly he's ready to take it for a spin? Sorry, hard pass."

"C'mon, X," Sage sings from the back seat.

X doesn't budge. "You must be out of your minds! That's Eddie behind the wheel, guys. He can't even drive a remote control car without getting into an accident."

I laugh. "Dude, I was seven years old. When you gonna let that go?"

"When you buy me a new remote control car! Hmph!" X shouts, turning his back to us, arms still folded across his chest. "I'm sorry, guys. You're gonna have to either figure out another way or go without me."

"You do remember I cut Mr. Bower's lawn with his riding mower, right?"

"His yard is the size of a board game. It's hard to mess that up!"

"You're right! And it's the same with this. Besides, there's no one else on the road. We'll be fine and I promise I'll drive even slower than your dad does."

X tries to keep a straight face but he caves just a little. "Leave my dad out of this."

Trey sticks his head out his window. "Come on, X. Let's go, man. We're a team."

"A family," Sage says. "And family sticks together."

X turns back toward us. "What? You think a super-awesome nine-year-old is gonna change my mind? Ha! Nope! Guess again!"

5300

X clicks his middle seat belt, his face on full frown mode.

"Aren't you so excited, X?" Sage asks from the comfort of her window seat.

"Remind me how I ended up in the middle seat again?" He's smushed into the back between Sage and Trey.

Sonia smiles. "Because you're not an ageist, bound to caveman rules whereby gender or age has no bearing on who gets what, because all of us are equal."

X begrudgingly nods. "Right. That."

I glance over at Sonia and then at the back seat—all their eyes focused in on me. "Are you guys ready to get our search party on?"

"You know it," Sonia says.

"Born ready," Sage adds.

"I'm pumped, my friend. Pumped," says Trey.

"Not really," X says. "But apparently what I want doesn't matter, so."

I laugh. "Well, good, I'm glad we're all on the same page. But there is one more thing we need to do before we go."

"What's up now?" Sonia asks as I pull out a bag from under my seat.

"These are for you. There's one for everybody," I say.

"Sunglasses?" Sage says. "We're like government agents or something!"

The kid has a point. It's pretty official. "We look good, if you ask me," I say to my four friends. "Even you, X."

"I can still get out the car," he shoots back. "It's not too late." The brake still on, I mash down on the gas and the engine roars and everyone's eyes grow as big as saucers. "See, I told you guys, he's reckless."

"X?" Sonia says. "You know I love you, but you gotta stop pooping on our party, bro."

X sighs extra hard. "Fine. Whatever. But just for the record, when this all goes bad, I'm the only one who had the good sense to vote against the part of the plan where Eddie Holloway drives us to our certain doom."

"Noted," Trey says, pretending to jot down X's objection in his nonexistent, air notebook.

"Well, then, if there are no further issues, you guys ready to take this show on the road?"

And everyone cheers, even X, who is doing it a lot softer than the rest of us.

I move the shifter out of park and into reverse, checking the back-up camera and using my side mirrors to check the road behind me.

"Um, what are you doing, dude? What are you waiting for?"

"Safety first, X. Gotta make sure I don't run over any pedestrians or pull out into oncoming traffic," I insist.

X looks over both shoulders. "I think you're good."

"No, no, you were right before, X. We don't wanna take anything for granted, especially our lives. No, better safe than sorry." And I take my time checking every mirror multiple times to make sure everything's cool, yes, but also to annoy X.

It's wild—how in such a short time, everything you know can change. How everyone you know can disappear in the blink of an eye.

I think it's safe to say I had some large expectations about this weekend.

Yep, as far as I was concerned, yesterday was supposed to be the best day Eddie Gordon Holloway has ever had. I woke up extra happy. Popped out of bed so ecstatic that my head nearly missiled through the roof. That never happens.

I'd waited half the summer for what I knew would be the party of the whole year. I'd even devised the perfect plan to avoid laundry—with my very last shred of clean clothing being these swim trunks, my bathing suit.

And yet somehow absolutely zero of those things happened.

Literally not one.

Which is wild, right? I mean forty summer days' worth of planning and anticipation for one single day all goes to waste.

I thought that Beach Bash would change me.

That everything would be better, yes, but also bolder and brighter.

Maybe I'd never be the most popular kid in school—or

considered one of the cool kids—but at Beach Bash, I was finally gonna get my chance to shine. To show everyone just how cool I could be. Which was ridiculously dumb.

Because it turns out the regular old Eddie Gordon Holloway? He's not so bad. Especially with his super friends at his side.

"OMG, really, my dude? Seriously, are you still checking your mirrors?" X complains, which makes everyone laugh, because one of my favorite things about X is how easy the dude gets so stressed.

"Annnnnndddd, safety checks are complete." I wink at him through the rearview mirror. "Let's do this."

"Time for this bird to fly the coop," Sage says with a grin. "Get it? Thunderbird . . . coop?" And X groans, but me, I turn to give her a high five because I'm never not here for the dad jokes.

X rubs both sides of his forehead. "Why do I get the feeling we're gonna majorly regret this?"

And I shrug, my smile brightening as I lift my foot and release the brake. "You won't regret it any more than we all regret your haircut."

We all bust out laughing; there's even something smile-ish

hanging out on Mr. Grinch's, ahem, I mean X's, lips. "Have I told you how much I hate you all?" X says.

Sonia coos, reaching back to rub the good half of X's head. "Awwww, did you guys hear that? X loves us soooo much."

And I smile as I shift the car into drive. "Of course he does. What's not to love?"

An extremely brief closing note from our storytelling master, Eddie Gordon Holloway, who just hooked you all the way up:

Wait, hold up, hold up. Now I know you guys didn't really think I'd leave you hanging like that? That I'd just dip without saying goodbye? C'mon, haven't I kept my word to you? Haven't I hooked you up this entire time? Made sure you had everything you needed AND gave you some killer advice on how to maximize your fun along the way? No, no, you don't gotta thank me. I know you'd do the same for me. Because we're friends, right? And that's what friends do, yeah? We look out for each other. We crack jokes on each other. And no matter what, we never, ever leave without saying good—

Bahahaha, got yaaa! Admit it, you thought I bounced! For real, you should see your face right now—looking like the electricity just went out on you in my creepy basement—classic!

Anyway, I gotta get back to my other friends—they're kinda waiting for me, so I'm gonna catch up with y'all later, cool? So until next time, see you when I see you, and remember, don't do anything I wouldn't do, which, seeing how the list of things I wouldn't do is only like two things—commit a crime or share a room with The Bronster—that should still leave you with plenty of awesome options to pass the time, haha. So, go. What are you waiting for? Go live your life! Go explore! Go have fun!

Ciao! Deuces! Adiós! Peace!

Oh, wait, don't they usually say something at the end of a movie when the movie's over but like not really over?

You know what I'm talking about.

Wait, I got it. It's something like:

To beeeee continuuuued . . .

Yeah, I like that.

To be continued.

Because this here? This ain't over.

Not even close, my friends.

Trust me, we're just getting started.

THE END!

(but not really)

ACKNOWLEDGMENTS

First of all, thanks to all the readers, especially young people. You are *why* I write, craft, and dream. You are the future and the now. Be yourselves, always! Remember, your voice matters!

Thank you to all the parents, librarians—hi, Mom!—teachers, educators, counselors, and therapists, who are making sure this next generation gets the best start possible. I can't imagine a more important "job." You wear so many hats, and it's challenging to be so many things to so many kids, but you're doing it with style, integrity, and grace.

Big thanks to my editor and friend, Matt Ringler. We've long since talked about working on a project together, combining what we love most about movies, books, sports, and music. This book represents the culmination of lots of jokes, random conversations, and our stubborn insistence on tapping back into the "imagination of our youth." This book doesn't exist without you. '90s group pose forever! Also, you never told me what you did with that check you found in the park, haha . . .

Special thanks to super agent and friend, Beth Phelan. Thanks for protecting me from my overeager, overly ambitious self, haha. Thanks for being a great sounding board and a brilliant strategist, and for the perfect blend of tough (and soft) love!

Ginormous thanks to my family, for whom I work hard and love harder. Thank you for keeping it real, always—albeit maybe *too* real sometimes, haha. Thank you for telling me *I can* when it feels like *I can't*. Thank you for listening to my *I just had this idea* rambles at all hours. Thank you for letting me be corny and sleepy and hype and eager. Thank you for dealing with my sometimes-annoying spontaneity and propensity for long speeches. I love you tenaciously.

Huge thanks to my friends, without whom my world would be gray. Thank you for injecting beautiful, bold color—even when I don't think I want it, haha—via laughs and memes and well-timed texts. Thanks for our grumpy miscellaneous complaint sessions, haha. Most of all, thank you for your immense understanding, support, and compassion. I hope I'm half the friend and human all of you are!

Super thanks to all the "behind-the-scenes" humans who help turn my random ideas and thoughts into this thing of beauty—yeah, I'm looking at you, copyeditor extraordinaire, Starr Baer; super-talented proofreaders, Priscilla Eakeley, Jackie Hornberger, and Jan Arzooman. And big thanks to all the other incredibly important and relentlessly good people at Scholastic who make things happen: Stephanie Yang, Janell Harris, Jazan Higgins, Alex Kelleher-Nagorski, Abigail McAden, Mariclaire Jastremsky, Elizabeth Whiting, Ellie Berger, and David Levithan. Thank you for believing in me. For advocating for *all* kids.

A special thank-you to Maya Marlette for picking up this baton, and for running full speed with heart and humor.

Thanks to Celia Lee for being this end-of-the-world idea's first champion!

Shout-out to my therapist for holding me down; it means a lot. I've been thinking, though, about how I give you free tech advice— I hope your son enjoys those headphones!—and I'm thinking we should discuss a discount; like maybe one hour of my tech savvy equates to thirty minutes of your brain expertise. How does that make you feel, haha.

Thanks to Cleveland and LL for being the perfect backdrop to my stories. Best city on earth, fight me! ☺

And finally, thank you, Eddie, for giving voice to all my laundry disdain! Honestly, my only real issue is I *loathe* putting clean laundry away, but still, I appreciate your whole vibe. Never change! I mean, change as in "grow in empathy, love, and wisdom"—and probably height, too—but other than that, stay you!

Okay, that's it. What are you sticking around here for? Go read another book! ☺

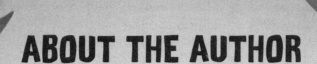

ABOUT THE AUTHOR

justin a. reynolds has always wanted to be a writer. *Opposite of Always*, his debut novel, was an Indies Introduce selection and a *School Library Journal* Best Book, has been translated into seventeen languages, and is being developed for film with Paramount Players. He hangs out in Northeast Ohio with his family and likes it, and is probably somewhere, right now, dancing terribly. His second novel, *Early Departures*, published September 2020, and his third novel, *Miles Morales: Shock Waves*, published June 2021. You can find him at justinareynolds.com.